The Day
the Music Died

Books by Ed Gorman

The Jack Dwyer Series

New, Improved Murder • *Murder Straight Up* •
Murder in the Wings • *The Autumn Dead* •
A Cry of Shadows

The Tobin Series

Murder on the Aisle • *Several Deaths Later*

The Robert Payne Series

Blood Moon • *Hawk Moon* • *Harlot's Moon*

Suspense Novels

The Night Remembers • *Night Kills* • *Black River Falls*

Thrillers

The Marilyn Tapes • *The First Lady* • *Runner in the
Dark* • *Senatorial Privilege*

Short Story Collections

Prisoners • *Cages* • *Dark Whispers* • *Moonchasers*

The Day the Music Died

A Mystery

ED GORMAN

CARROLL & GRAF PUBLISHERS, INC.
NEW YORK

I'd like to thank the staff at the Emma Goldman Clinic for answering all my interminable questions.

Carroll & Graf Publishers, Inc.
19 West 21st Street
New York, NY 10010-6805

ISBN: 0-7867-0569-8

Manufactured in the United States of America

To Roz, Madeline and Marty—
the Greenbergs of Green Bay—
with fondness, gratitude and love

He wasn't really happy; he was only watching happiness from close to instead of from far away.

—Graham Greene, "The Basement Room"

The Day
the Music Died

PART I

ONE

S HE DIDN'T SAY MUCH after we left the Surf Ballroom that
night, Pamela Forrest.

Which meant one of three things. (1) She didn't like Buddy
Holly nearly as much as I did. (2) She was worried 'bout the long
trip back to Black River Falls on the wintry roads of February 3,
1959. (3) She was thinking about Stu Grant, the wealthy young
man she'd been in love with since ninth grade, the only problem
being that I'd been in love with *her* since fourth grade.

Or maybe it was my ragtop that made her silent. She knew
how much I prized my 1951 red Ford convertible with the custom skirts, the louvered hood and the special weave top. The
trouble was, despite the custom convertible top, the Ford could
get pretty cold when the night winds blew across the dead Iowa
cornfields, and the head-winds were enough to push the car into
the next lane every once in a while. There was a bad snowstorm
around the area of the ballroom. It took us forty-five minutes to
drive out of it.

I had the noisy heater on full tilt and as a consequence I had to
turn the radio way up to be heard over the heater. I was playing
the rock and roll station out of Oklahoma City, KOMA: 100,000
clear-channel watts of pure pleasure. Gene Vincent was on now,

and there was the promise of Little Richard's new song within the half hour. We had a three-and-a-half hour drive ahead of us, so I was going to need all the rock and roll I could get.

"You think we could change the station?" the lovely Pamela Forrest finally said.

"The station?"

"Please. That stuff's giving me a headache."

"Gee, then tonight must have been terrible for you. You should've said something."

"I knew how much it meant to you, McCain, seeing Buddy Holly and those other people. I didn't want to spoil it for you."

"Then you didn't even like Holly?"

She sighed. "Don't take this the wrong way, McCain, but I still like Perry Como better." Then, "And Stu's teaching me about opera. That's what he listens to all the time. That, and classical music."

"Good ole Stu."

"I told you, didn't I, that he was nominated for Outstanding Young Lawyer of the Year, didn't I?"

"Yeah, I dimly recall you mentioning it six or seven thousand times."

"That doesn't mean you're not a good lawyer, McCain."

"I'll try and remember that."

"Or that you won't be a judge someday yourself."

"Who said he was going to be a judge?"

"Well, how's he ever going to get on the Supreme Court if he isn't a judge first?"

Good old Stu. Modesty had never been a problem for him.

I couldn't take talking about Stu's plan to become the Supreme Ruler of the Known Universe anymore, so I changed the station. I couldn't find Perry Como for her. But I did find Jerry Vale and some other crooners. This seemed to satisfy her. She snuggled up on her side of the car, her astonishingly lovely legs up on the seat and covered with her long, brown coat. She stared out the window.

Despite a full moon, there wasn't much to see. After a snowfall

like the one we'd had the past two days, rural Iowa in the moonlight looks like the surface of an alien world—long, white, empty
stretches of land where the wind stirs up dust devils of chill snow
every once in a while. The only signs of life are the distant lights
of snug little farmhouses tucked in windbreaks of oak trees or
jack pine. Every once in a while, there'd be what they call a
hamlet, a block or so of darkened buildings, usually a co-op and
a general store and a gas station. There might be a tavern open,
Johnny Cash brooding and lonely and dangerous in the prairie
night. Then darkness again as you hit the highway, the hamlet
suddenly vanished, like a dream on waking.

"You aren't, you know, *expecting* anything are you tonight,
McCain?"

"Nah."

"Because I was very careful not to mislead you."

"I know."

"It's nothing personal."

"Sure, it's personal," I said. "But it's not *personal* personal."

She laughed. "Boy, you say some strange things sometimes."

After about forty miles, the heater started to do some good. I
wished I could do some good. I'd tried several conversation start-
ers but none of them had worked. She'd mutter something in
return, then go back to staring out the window.

I said, "So if you don't like rock and roll, why'd you go tonight?"

I guess you pretty much know the answer I wanted. The one
where she'd say, "Because I just wanted to be alone with you,
McCain."

Instead, she said, "Because I owe you for helping me move."

"Oh."

"That was hard work."

"Oh."

"So I just figured I should pay you back."

Two weeks ago, on very short notice, she'd had the chance to
move into an apartment in the old Belding mansion. The apartment had a fireplace, veranda and large living room. She needed

help. I offered my services and those of Leonard Dubois, Leonard being one of my legal clients. I got him a bench parole for his earnest attempt to become a burglar and he's been grateful ever since. Not grateful enough to pay me, of course, so I figured I might as well get some work out of him. We spent all day Saturday and half a day Sunday getting Pamela moved in. It didn't rain half as much as predicted. Both days when we finished, I asked Leonard to empty his pockets. He only stole stuff on Saturday. I guess by Sunday he'd learned his lesson. Maybe this is what rehabilitation means.

About halfway home, Pamela put her feet on the floor and her head against the back of the seat and went to sleep. She snored, but not loudly, and sometimes she whistled when she snored, like a teakettle. It was cute and it made me sentimental about her and when I get sentimental about her, I get scared because then I realize that I'm probably going to be in love with her the rest of my life. It's hard to figure, why I'm in love with her, I mean. Her grandfather's wealth had been lost in the Depression. Her parents were forced to live in the Knolls for several years, but they always drove their shiny eight-year-old Packard and always managed to get themselves invited to country club dos. And there was Pamela, beautiful little yearning eight-year-old Pamela, too good for us in the Knolls but not good enough for the rich kids. And I guess I kind of felt sorry for her or something because one day I woke up and I was in love with her and it was like an incurable disease there was no cure for.

She started talking in her sleep. It was very earnest, the talk, but I had no idea what she was saying. And then she was awake. For a moment, she looked disoriented, lost. Then, she said, "Oh" and sat back again and stared out the window.

"You were dreaming."

"Yes."

"You were talking, too."

"Yes, I remember. To my mom. I was telling her that we were rich again. She used to tell me what it was like to walk downtown on Saturday morning with Granddad, how big and handsome he was. She said he was nice, too, always giving people money when he felt they deserved it. He'd been poor when he was a kid. She said it was really neat, walking down the street with him and people smiling at them and tipping their hats and stuff like that." Then her voice got teary. "I'd just like to be able to tell her before she dies that we're rich again. I love her so much." Her mother had a heart condition. The prognosis wasn't good.

We got into Black Rivers Falls, population 26,750 or thereabouts, around three in the morning. I drove straight through the business district. Most of the stores had been built in the twenties and thirties. There were a lot of gargoyles and Roman numerals chipped into the stone and concrete. The snow-covered city park was fronted by the statue of a Yankee general who was now used as target practice by militaristic pigeons, and the octagonal bandstand had been defaced by the chalked name of various rock stars including, my god, Pat Boone. But the modern world was here, too, a shiny red Corvette in the window of Daniels' Chevrolet and an Edsel in the window of Loomis' Ford, Tony Curtis and Rock Hudson on the marquee of the Avalon. Even the taverns were dark. An overhead red light was getting whipped around pretty good in the windy intersection and snow was starting to stick on the sidewalks.

Pamela woke up. "God, Judge Whitney's going to kill me if I have dark rings under my eyes. You know how she gets."

"Tell her it's none of her business."

She smiled sleepily. "Right, McCain. That's just how *you'd* handle it, isn't it? You're more afraid of her than I am."

Which was true, I guess. As a young lawyer in a town that already had too many lawyers, I earned more than 60 percent of my income as an investigator for Judge Esme Anne Whitney. I'd even taken two years worth of criminology courses at the U of Iowa in Iowa City so I could be even more help to the judge, making the forty-mile roundtrip three nights a week until I became the proud owner of my private investigator's license. But to earn any money with that license, I had to stay on Judge

Whitney's good side. Assuming, despite a lot of evidence to the contrary, that she actually *had* a good side.

The Belding mansion is on Winthrop Avenue, which is where the wealthy of the town first settled. The estates run to three-acre lawns, carriage houses and native stone mansions that have a castlelike air about them. The Belding mansion was big enough to have a moat. But now it was broken up into apartments for "proper" working girls.

I drove through the open iron gates right up to the wide front steps. It was like dropping a girl off at her college dorm.

She leaned over and kissed me on the cheek, a rustle of skirt and blouse and coat, a seductive scent of perfume. "Sorry, I wasn't more fun. You really should find a girl, McCain."

I started to say something, then she said, "It's Stu's birthday. I guess I was preoccupied with that a little bit. That's why I didn't talk more."

"He's engaged, Pamela. I'm not engaged. I just thought I'd point that out."

She shook her head. She has the quiet beauty of the past century, those huge blue eyes and the wide serious mouth that can break into a girly smile with devastating ease. "He won't marry her."

"He won't?"

"He told me he won't. He said he only got engaged because he's running for governor in four years and the Republican steering committee said it'd look better if he was engaged. That's why he got his pilot's license, too. So people wouldn't just write him off as a rich boy. He flies sick kids up to the Mayo Clinic all the time, remember."

"I wonder if she knows that. His fiancée. Why he got engaged to her."

"The point is, McCain. He loves me, not her."

"And he told you that?"

"Yes, of course he told me that. In fact, he tells me that twice a week. When he calls."

What we had here was a young man afraid to displease his

folks. Pamela and I grew up in a hilly area north of town called the Knolls. You find a lot of junked cars in the front yards of the Knolls, and at least twice a night, a red siren comes blazing up there, usually to stop a man from beating up his wife and to arrest a teenager who thought that smashing car windows was a Junior Achievement project. Most of the lives there are like the junked cars in the front yards.

This is not the kind of background Stu's parents wanted to add to their family history, even if the girl did look a lot like Grace Kelly. Stu loved Pamela but he loved his parents and his social situation more. Pamela didn't seem to understand this. She'd learned how to dress, how to speak, how to act, how to tell one kind of fork from the other, and she felt that would be enough for Stu. But it wasn't enough for his folks, and never would be.

She got out and, for the moment, the door was open. The night air felt good, clear and purifying somehow.

I watched Pamela's good legs flash going up the steps and then she was gone, and I just sat there inhaling her perfume and remembering what it was like to walk her home from high school on Indian summer afternoons. My life had been so complete at those moments. She was all I'd ever wanted, dreamed of. I wanted that sense of completeness again. I wanted to be fifteen again and have it all ahead for us, for both of us, only this time there'd be no Stu. There'd just be us. Just us.

TWO

THE CALL CAME AFTER I'd been asleep for about two hours. I woke dazed and confused, the way you get when you're sleeping off whiskey. Not that I get that way very often. Two drinks, I go to sleep. Three drinks, I generally throw up. My dad's the same way. Heredity, I guess. For the sake of everybody concerned, I mostly stick to Pepsi.

A sunny dawn sky was at the windows of my apartment, bare black branches like antlers on the panes. I cleared my throat and said hello.

"I'm sorry to bother you, McCain, but I need you to throw your clothes on and get out to Kenny's place."

She didn't need to identify herself. There was only one voice like hers in the entire state. Not only was it imperious, it was somehow Eastern too—Smith College, I think—though she'd lived here all her life, Judge Esme Anne Whitney.

Tasha and Crystal, my cats, were lost among the muss of winter covers, yawning and stretching and deeply resenting being awakened at this time. I'm not a cat guy, actually. Samantha, a local community college drama star, left them with me when she went to Hollywood to become a movie star. She writes me every six months or so to tell she'll be sending for them as soon as director Billy Wilder gives her a part. She's fixated on Billy Wilder. Meanwhile, I have the cats, and, worst of all, I've started to consider them family. I know guys aren't supposed to like cats (out here, you still occasionally find the stout masculine type who goes out and *shoots* cats), but I can't help it. They've won me over.

"Does it have to be right now, Judge?" I almost asked, "I just got to sleep." Then I stopped myself. If I admitted to being out that late, I'd not only have to get dressed, I'd have to listen to a sermon while I was fumbling around with my clothes and shoes.

"Eight hours' sleep should be plenty for an active young man like yourself, McCain."

"Yes, I guess it should."

"Kenny seems to be having some kind of difficulty."

"Your nephew, Kenny?"

"Yes, my nephew, Kenny. I know you two don't like each other much but he seems to be—hysterical."

Her nephew, Kenny, had given me my one and only shiner. Eleventh grade. Mr. Stearns' civics class. Kenny and I had started arguing about civil rights. Kenny had a vast ship upon which he wanted to put all Negroes, non-English speakers, atheists, union members, communists, Jews, Catholics and people who'd ever refused to cooperate with the House on Un-American Activities. He inherited his beliefs from his father, Judge Whitney's brother, who was head of the local bar association. I made a few points that got Kenny snickered at. One thing a Whitney can't abide is being ridiculed. Kenny waited for me in the parking lot, in full view of Pamela Forrest. Kenny was starting fullback for our Wilson Warriors. I stood five-seven and weighed 130 pounds. Hence, my black eye, and my humiliation in front of Pamela.

"I'm not sure I'm the right man for this, Judge."

"He won't hurt you."

"I know he won't hurt me. I'm bringing my forty-five if I go."

"Are you serious?"

"Damned right, I'm serious. But I still don't think I'm the right man."

"You may not be the right man but you're the *only* man I can reach. Now get out there."

I reached over and petted Tasha, who was an elegant tabby. Then I stroked Crystal, a black-and-white beauty with a Disney profile. "You could always call Cliff Sykes."

"Are you always this hilarious at five seventeen A.M.?"

"I'm at my *most* hilarious at five seventeen A.M."

Cliff Sykes is the local police chief. For four generations, Whitney money ran this town. Then Sykes, Sr., got rich during WWII building training facilities for the Army–Air Force. Now Sykes money runs the town. Judge Whitney always refers to him as "that damned hillbilly" and she isn't far wrong.

"Get out there, McCain, and find out what's going on. He sounded pretty bad."

"His house?"

"His house."

Then she hung up.

I decided to wear my pink shirt from last night. You remember a couple of years ago when everything went pink? Well, I went right along with it. I am the proud owner of three pink dress shirts and the damned things never seem to fade, frazzle, stain or wear out. I am happy to report, however, that I do not own a pink tie, pink socks or a pink sport coat. Moderation in everything.

I shaved, took what my mom always called a sponge bath (face, neck, pits, crotch, backside with a soapy washcloth), went heavy on the Old Spice, easy on the Wildroot hair cream.

As I got dressed, I called Val's Diner and had them put up a three-cup paper container of coffee for me. I picked it up on the way out of town. The local gravel roads being what they are, I had a nice soaked spot right in my crotch. Pretty smart, putting a coffee container between my legs as I sped over roads so rough your voice trembled when you talked. Not for nothing did I toil in the intellectual fields of the University of Iowa.

I was a couple of miles out of town—racing along under several Air Force jets whose direction indicated that they'd probably come from Norfolk, Nebraska, where there was a base, which I was personally thankful for, given the fact that I just assumed someday Mother Russia would drop the atomic bomb—when the word came on the radio news.

Plane crash. Buddy Holly. Richie Valens. Big Bopper. Taking off from the town where we'd seen them at the Surf Ballroom last night. It's odd how we are about celebrities. We invent them to suit ourselves and they stay that way until the press gives us a good reason to think otherwise. I liked Buddy Holly because he was kind of gawky and I liked Richie Valens because he was Mexican. They didn't fit in and I've never fit in either. So they were more than really great rock and rollers, they were guys I identified with. I was tired and then I was sad for two guys I'd never really known, and I thought of how my aunt had been that day in 1944 when she learned that my uncle had been killed in Italy, her just sitting at my folks' kitchen table with a bottle of Pabst and a pack of Chesterfields and the Andrews Sisters on the record player in the living room, a woman who never drank or smoked, just sitting there and staring out the warm open April window, staring and saying nothing, nothing at all even when the day cooled and became dusk, even when the dusk darkened and became night, saying nothing at all.

THREE

Six years ago, Kenny Whitney had married one of the most beautiful girls in the valley, and set her up inside the huge Tudor-style home he'd built for her, and expected her to stay happy while he went right on with his single style of life. Lots of whiskey. Lots of poker. Lots of fights. Lots of girls.

The house was eight miles southeast of town. Some of the rural mailboxes still wore their Christmas decorations. The cows in the barnyards exhaled steamy breath that joined with the vapor that rose from their cow pies. The chimneys of the farmhouses all had snakes of gray smoke uncoiling into the blue sky, and here and there yellow school buses were picking up shivering little kids hugging books and lunch pails. My own personal pride and joy had been a Roy Rogers lunch pail, with Roy's arm slung around Trigger's neck and a six-gun dangling from his fingers. That was until Hopalong Cassidy appeared on the TV screen in 1948. Kids are fickle. I went all out for Hoppy. Hat, shirt, jeans, socks, boots, six-shooters and, if I'm not mistaken, underwear. Who'd be crazy enough to go anywhere without his Hoppy underwear?

Nothing remarkable about the Tudor. No cars visible on the long drive or on the apron of the three-stall garage. No tire tracks in the light snow that had dusted the town last night, nobody in or out for some time. Then I noticed the chimney, the only chimney I'd seen this morning without smoke.

I swung into the drive. Nothing moved. I sat in the ragtop scouting out this side of the house. I didn't notice the frost at first. I did notice the downstairs window that was missing a pane, jagged edges of glass rimming the interior of the frame, the kind of damage caused by something hurled through the window.

A sweet-faced border collie came around the far side of the garage. She looked hungry and scared and lost, sniffing the ground. She came over to the car and I opened the door. Even in the cold, she smelled sweetly canine. I got out of the ragtop and rubbed the collie's face lightly, trying to get her warm. The temperature was somewhere around ten degrees above zero.

My new friend stayed right with me all the way across the back drive, right up until somebody poked a rifle out of an upstairs window and fired at me.

The collie jerked away to the right and I threw myself on the snow and started rolling to the left.

Then the second shot exploded.

The criminology and police courses I took at the University of Iowa weren't all held in the classrooms. We'd spent a week at the police academy in Des Moines and had learned a number of things about facing down an armed opponent. I even did pretty well in boxing, which was an elective you could take at night.

I had my .45 out and had rolled flat against the house, over some prickly bushes. He'd have a hard time getting me in range from the upstairs window now.

In town, the rifle shots would attract instant attention. Out here they'd simply be attributed to a hunter.

"Get the hell off my land," he shouted. No mistaking the voice. Kenny Whitney. King of the world. Just ask him.

"Your aunt sent me."

"I don't care who sent you. You don't get off my land, I've got the right to shoot you."

"I hate to tell you this, but that isn't how the law works, Kenny."

"Yeah, well, then maybe it's how the law should work."

I stood up and brushed myself off. Unless I stepped away from the house, I was safe. "I want to talk to you, Kenny."

"You go to hell."

Then something strange happened. There was a silence, a long one, and then I heard a man sobbing. Kenny was crying. Out here in the boonies, a beautiful if cold sunny day, the chink of tire chains in the distance, a big United plane coming in low, preparing to land in Cedar Rapids—and Kenny Black-Eye Whitney was crying. I probably should have enjoyed the sound, hearing him as vulnerable as the rest of us humans. But it cut into me, that sound, the grief and horror in it. And then the shot came and I didn't have any doubt who the target was. The target was Kenny himself.

FOUR

THE BACK DOOR WAS LOCKED. I smashed one of the fractional windowpanes with the butt of my .45, then reached inside past the cotton curtains and found the doorknob. I pushed on the door and followed it inward.

I'd always been curious about the place—every year the local paper ran a photo spread on its most recent improvements—but now wasn't the time to pause and gawk. I needed to get upstairs.

But I only got as far as the living room. Susan lay on her back on the floor. She wore a modest white terry-cloth robe. There was blood all over the front of it. There was blood on her face, too. The bottoms of her feet were dirty. I don't know why I noticed that, but I did. It's the kind of thing doctors record at autopsies. They'd made some pretty crude jokes, the times I'd sat in. I'd wanted to defend the dead people they were making fun of. Maybe it's the lawyer in me.

My first impulse was to kneel down, check her out. But what was the point? By the looks of things, she was long dead. Her face was starting to discolor badly.

Silence from upstairs. Maybe he'd pulled it off. He'd been lucky at everything else. Why not lucky at his suicide attempt?

I went upstairs, moving carefully. If he wasn't dead, he might want to start shooting at me again. The stairway was enclosed. I took the steps slowly, carefully, and when I reached the top, I smelled floor polish. And then the fresh smell of rifle fire. The floor creaked as I stepped on to the hallway. Two doors on one side, three on the other. I gripped my .45 harder, feeling self-conscious. You see so much gunplay on private eye TV shows that you think it feels natural to have a gun in your hand. But it doesn't. You're carrying such quick-and-easy death in your hand. There's so much responsibility, and fear. At least for me.

A bathroom. Watery blood smeared all over the white porcelain sink. A bedroom that I sensed—given its neatness and slightly impersonal accoutrements—was a guest room. Another bathroom, this one huge compared to the other one. And then another bedroom. Or a monument to bedrooms. This had everything, including a large TV, stereo speakers on the wall and yet another bathroom. Everything in this bedroom was sumptuous, from the carpeting to the silver-handled hairbrushes on the dressing table. This was how rich people lived, at least around here. Except for the two fresh bullet holes in the ceiling and the raw smell of cordite. He hadn't done so well by his suicide attempt.

I was just turning around to leave the bedroom when I saw him in the doorway. I hadn't seen him in some time and at first I hardly recognized him. The chiseled face was fleshy now, as was his waistline. The eyes were alarming, tinted red from sleeplessness and whiskey and grief, and underscored with deep dark half-moons of loose and wrinkled flesh. His hair had started to thin. He was my age. This kind of aging didn't just happen; you had to go out and earn it. The white oxford button-down shirt he wore had traces of blood on the sleeves and the cuffs. His chinos showed even more blood. His feet were bare.

He held a Remington hunting rifle on me. He said, "I've got some whiskey downstairs."

Then he quietly laid the rifle against the door frame and led the way back down the hallway to the stairs.

FIVE

H E LED ME THROUGH the dining room so we didn't have
to see the body of his wife in the living room.

In the kitchen, he pointed to the breakfast nook and then he
opened a cupboard door and pulled down a fresh bottle of Cana-
dian Club. He slit the seal with his thumbnail. He grabbed two
glasses, opened the refrigerator and the freezer compartment and
got out a small bowl of ice, and then carried everything over to
the breakfast nook where I was sitting. I'd put my .45 away. It
had started to feel awfully melodramatic.

As he poured and noisily dumped in some ice cubes, I looked
out the window at a squirrel wrestling with an acorn it had found
on the sunny snow. The border collie was back, too, sniffing my
tires.

"Sweetest dog I've ever owned," Kenny Whitney said. He
smiled sadly. "Wish I had her personality." His voice startled me.
I associated Kenny with the quick, derisive jab, making you feel
bad for being unpopular or ugly or fat or sissy, at least in his eyes.
And for short, barked threats. He was a master at short, barked
threats. But this was a slow and considered voice, and it was an
adult voice. That's what startled me most. He looked a lot older
than he should have, but he'd turned into an adult in the process.

"Why the hell'd you shoot at me?"

He shook his head, "Sorry. I was just crazy is all I can say. I wasn't really trying to hit you, though."

"You came close enough."

"I should never have called her. Gotten her involved."

He leaned his head against the back of the nook. The kitchen sparkled. The appliances were brand-new and sat there basking in their own suburban glory. Then he sat up straight and wrapped a massive fullback's hand around his glass. He drained the whole drink in a single swallow and then filled up again with the bottle he'd just opened. "You see her in there?"

"Yeah."

"You call Sykes yet?"

"I wanted to make sure you were still alive."

"Oh. I'm alive. Unfortunately."

"You kill her, Kenny?"

He looked up at me. "Yeah."

I let out a long sigh. "When?"

"Early last night. We were both pretty drunk."

"What happened?"

"She wanted a divorce. I didn't."

"So you shot her?"

He stared at me for a long time. "Yeah."

"Don't tell me anything more."

"Why not?"

"Because you need a lawyer."

"I don't suppose you'd want that honor?"

I smiled at him. "Kenny, I don't like you. I've never liked you. Believe me, you don't want me for a lawyer."

"I guess I was kind of a jerk back in school, wasn't I?"

"You remember my black eye?"

He shrugged. "Not really. I mean, I gave a lot of guys black eyes."

"Well, you gave me mine right in front of Pamela Forrest."

He looked at me and grinned. "Oh, yeah, now I remember.

Not your black eye. But Pamela. Man, you really made a fool of yourself over her."

"I guess I did."

His face became dour and old again. "Well, join the club, my friend. That's the problem Susan and I were having. And that's one of the reasons I killed her. She was running around on me."

"Running around on you? God, look how you ran around on her."

He was pouring himself his third drink. His third drink since we'd sat down, anyway. He'd had many more during the night. "You need to keep up on the town gossip, McCain. I quit running around on her over two years ago. I even went on the wagon. She'd threatened to leave me and then I realized how much I loved her. Then she fell in love with somebody else."

"Don't tell me anything more. Save it for your lawyer."

"All I was going to say was that when she asked me for a divorce last night, I couldn't handle it. I took down a bottle of whiskey—I'd gotten used to having it around, you know, for when we had company and stuff—and then I really started knocking down the drinks. After two years of being dry, they really hit me hard."

"So then you killed her?"

He shrugged again. "Then I killed her."

The funny thing was, I didn't believe him. "Why're you telling me this?"

"That I killed her? Because it's the truth. We may as well get it over with. With Sykes and all. Man, will that hillbilly be gloating. He'll actually have a member of Judge Whitney's family in his jail. He'll probably play Webb Pierce records all day long." Webb Pierce was the country-western favorite of the moment. A small Iowa town like this, people liked to show their sophistication by shunning country music. Badge of honor.

"I still want to know why you're telling me this."

"I told you. Because I just want to get it over with. It's pretty obvious that I killed her, isn't it?" Then he drained off his drink.

I stood up. "I'm going to walk over to the phone and call Sykes."

"Fine. That's what I want you to do."

"I'm also going to call Bob Tompkins for you. He's the best criminal attorney in this part of the state. Your aunt has a lot of respect for him."

He looked at me abruptly. "I don't want to have to see her again."

I wasn't sure who he meant. "Who?"

"You know. Susan."

"Okay." Then, "It's freezing in here."

"Yeah, after I shot her, I guess I went a little nuts. I smashed out some windows and stuff."

I still didn't believe he'd killed her and I still didn't know why. I went to the phone and called Cliff Sykes, Jr., and listened to him try to hide his glee. Then I called Judge Whitney and repeated what I'd told Sykes. I also told her I'd like to invite Bob Tompkins in. She said she thought that was a good idea.

I had just hung up when the shot sounded. I glanced at the empty breakfast nook behind me. I had a feeling he'd been better at it this time. A kind of sorrow came over me, one I hadn't counted on driving out here. I'd always hated him and with good reason. But he'd been sad this morning, human-animal sad, a creature frenzied and forlorn and crazed, and he wouldn't let me hate him anymore, the son of a bitch, no matter how much I might have wanted to.

I went upstairs and found him on the bed. He looked even older now, a lot older.

SIX

TWO HOURS LATER, I got to play celebrity. I'd needed a haircut for two weeks so I walked from my tiny law office to Bill and Phil's. The walk helped; the cold air woke me up, the golden sunlight lent me an air of hope. Sometimes, I'd think about Pamela, sometimes I'd think about Kenny, and sometimes I'd think about Buddy Holly and Richie Valens.

Bill Malley gave me my first haircut when I was two or three. My folks have a photo of me sitting on a board stretched across the arms of his barber chair with his barber sheet drawn up to my neck. He always gave little kids suckers, the way dentists do. Adults, he just gives speeches. Bill's favorite topics are communism (he's against it), fluoride (he's against it), civil rights marches (he's against them), Senator McCarthy (he was for him) and Sammy Davis, Jr. (he's against him).

By rights, I should go to Phil, who's a Democrat like myself. But Phil has a halitosis problem that could melt a metal wall.

Both chairs were filled, one of them by Jim Truman. He was a handyman who worked out of his house on the edge of town, along a scenic leg of the Cedar River. The joke was that he wanted to be buried in an Osh-Kosh coffin because everything else he wore—cap, shirt, bib overalls—carried the Osh-Kosh label. He'd come here a few years ago after the Korean War, in which he'd lost his leg below the knee. Now he wore an artificial one. The Fix-It Man was what he had painted on the front of his trailer. He was a marvel of arcane knowledge and physical dexterity. He could fix everything from a blender to a car engine. He always said he couldn't fix TVs but folks knew that was because he didn't want to hurt Benny Welsh's business, Benny being the guy who first started selling and repairing TVs here in the late forties.

My celebrity was a result of my being at the Whitney place when Kenny took his life. I'd waited around for Sykes and his incompetents to show up, told them what I knew, then headed back for town.

When I got done repeating my account for the boys in the barbershop, Bill said, "Probably fluoride."

"Huh?" I said.

"Sure," he said. "It rots your brain just the way the commies want it to."

"Ah," I said.

"Well, figure it out for yourself, Counselor," he said. A lot of people called me "counselor" as a joke, mostly because I've still got a baby face and freckles. "Guy brushes his teeth as much as Kenny did, and the water's got fluoride in it, how long before the guy goes psycho and kills somebody?"

Phil rolled his eyes. "There goes those commies workin' overtime again."

"Well, you laugh now, my friend, but someday when you see the mayor turned into a zombie and walkin' down the street with an ax in his hand—"

"Hell, the mayor's *already* a zombie," Phil said. "He don't need no fluoride to help him."

The men in the chair laughed. Bill and Phil had their mutual excoriation polished smooth as a vaudeville routine.

"Thanks for taking care of that contract for me," Jim Truman said. "I really appreciate it, Mr. McCain."

"My pleasure."

Truman had a long, angular face and brown eyes that had an almost cowlike docility, leading to the rumor that he might be slightly retarded in his deliberate, Osh-Kosh way. But he wasn't retarded. He just took his time, which was what made him such a good craftsman. He'd done a lot of home repairs for my folks and charged them about the fairest prices you could ask for.

Phil said, "They hear anything more about that girl?" to no one in particular. It was his way of starting us on a new topic of conversation.

"What girl?" I said dutifully.

"Next county over. Been missing four days now. Reason I asked, she's a shirttail cousin of one of my customers. He said she's a real nice little gal."

"Real nice little gal" translated to virginal. I like to sit in the barbershop and smell the hair oil and the talcum powder and the butch wax and the smoke from the various cigarettes, cigars and pipes. I like the friendship of the men and the sense you get when you have three or four generations of them sitting in the same room arguing about the Cubs or the Republicans or the latest scandal in Hollywood. An old-timer'll tell you about his Model-T, a WWII vet'll tell you what is was like in a Japanese concentration camp, somebody just back from Chicago'll tell you about the latest skyscraper going up. What I don't like is the local gossip, the cruelty of it. In a small town, you get punished for being different in any way, and sometimes when you sit in a small-town barbershop you get a sense of what Salem must have been like during the witch trials. Reputations get smeared, sometimes ruined permanently. Women get ripped up especially hard. A divorcée is inevitably a whore, and a widow is invariably a pent-up, frustrated sex machine. The modern version of the lynch mob: They hang you with innuendo and lies.

Jim Truman said, "Maybe she ran away."

Bill shook his head. "This cousin of hers says she wasn't the runnin'-away type."

Win Sullivan, the banker in Phil's chair, laughed and said,

"Maybe she ran into Sammy Davis, Jr., the way he's been stealin'
white gals lately."

Everybody laughed. Davis had been in the news for all his
affairs with white women. I always felt sorry for him. He was a
very talented guy but you could see how nervous and probably
scared he was. Three southerners had recently run up on the stage
where Nat King Cole was playing to a white audience and beaten
him up. America was a dangerous place for certain kinds of
people.

And so it went until it was finally my turn in the chair. I dozed
off and dreamed of the beautiful Pamela Forrest. We were out
canoeing on a gentle blue lake and she was telling me how much
she loved me.

"All done, Counselor," Bill said, waking me up.

No lake. No canoe. No Pamela.

I was out on the street again and the aftershave Bill had
slapped on stung pretty good in the February winds.

OVER THE NOON hour, at the Woolworth lunch counter and
the Rexall soda fountain and the courthouse cafeteria, the town
had a dilemma. They couldn't decide which they should talk
about first, the murder-suicide out at the Kenny Whitney place,
or the plane crash that killed Buddy Holly.

I was at Rexall having a ham sandwich and a cup of coffee,
and reading a new Peter Rabe paperback. I always sat at the far
end of the counter because that's where the metal paperback rack
was. It creaked rustily and threatened to fall over every time you
turned it. I usually read while I was eating. I was a big fan of
Gold Medal books. For twenty-five cents (plus a penny for the
governor, as folks in Iowa like to say), you could get the likes of a
brand-new novel by Rabe or Charles Williams or, my favorite,
John D. MacDonald. They were well-written, intelligent books,
too, despite the lurid covers. Of course, when you told people
that, they'd just wink at you and say, "Sure they are." Then

they'd nod to the cover with the seminaked girl and wink at you again.

"How about some more coffee?" a female voice asked. And I looked up into the pretty and almost impossibly sweet face of Mary Travers. Mary works days behind the counter at Rexall. She was the brightest girl in our class but her dad got throat cancer just before Mary started at the U of Iowa. She never did make it to college. Mary is the girl my mom and dad want me to marry and God, I wish I could make myself love her. A lot of times I get so mad at Pamela that I try to make myself love Mary.

We went out several times, even went to the county fair three nights running, and we ended up making out pretty passionately at the drive-in. Mary had loved me just about as long as I'd loved Pamela. She'd lived down the block from me up in the Knolls. I'd finally gone to the senior prom with her after it was clear that Pamela wasn't going at all because Stu Grant was going with someone else. I'd bought Mary a corsage and even managed to prevail upon an older cousin to buy me a pint of Jim Beam. He also gave me a rubber, a Trojan, and I hadn't even asked him for it. "Maybe you'll need it," he said. "It's Mary," I said. "I won't need it. I don't think of her that way." "Mary is beautiful, cuz. Every guy in town'd like to be with Mary, even if she is an egghead." But at the dance, the whiskey made me sad and I couldn't stop thinking of Pamela. Mary sensed this and then she got sad, too, and we ended up out at Tomahawk Park on the cliffs, drinking until we both got sick, and then just sitting there and listening to the wilder kids who were strewn all over the park in dark hideouts of delicious sin. A lot of girls were going to lose their virginity tonight. Senior prom night was the time to do it. I was sitting there smoking a Pall Mall and drinking one of the Pepsis that Mary had brought along. She handed me the Trojan. "It fell out of your pocket, McCain."

"Oh."

"I've never seen one before."

I was going to say something sophisticated—something Robert

Mitchum would say—you know, trying to impress her, but this was Mary. "I've seen them, but I've never used one before."

"Did you go in and buy it yourself?"

"Rolly kind of gave it to me."

"Did he kind of give you the whiskey, too?"

"Yeah."

"Russian hands and roamin' fingers," she said.

"Huh?"

"Your cousin," she said, "Rolly. I went on a hayrack ride with him one night. Talk about fast."

Then, "I'm sorry I threw up, McCain."

"Oh, that's all right. I threw up, too."

She said, "I mean maybe you were thinking we might—you know, use the rubber. I mean, I don't know if I'd actually have done it. But I guess now we'll never know."

I didn't say anything. She started to cry and I didn't know what to do and I sort of slid my arm around her and while I was doing it I could see down the front of her formal. She had small breasts but they were very sweet. I mean there's all kinds of breasts when you think about it, noisy breasts and quiet breasts and angry breasts and melancholy breasts and sincere breasts and superficial breasts and arrogant breasts and shy breasts and probably lots of other kinds, too; her breasts were just very sweet, like Mary herself. I guess that was the first time I wanted to love her. I mean I couldn't love her, not in the way she wanted me to, because I loved Pamela that way. But right then, if God had given me a choice, I would've said reach in my brain and take Pamela out and put Mary in. Because it would've made her so happy if I could have loved her that way. Pamela didn't care if I loved her at all. But Mary would have been all shiny and new and fine with it, just a few stupid words that you hear on the jukebox all the time, and she would have been so happy. So I held her and I kissed her and then we really started kissing and then we started rolling around on the grass and then it got real serious and while we didn't use the Trojan, we came damned close, damned close, and then we were in my older brother's 1946 Plymouth and headed out on the highway to where there was supposed to be a beer party at the old quarry and the radio was blasting Gene Vincent and Carl Perkins and the prairie night air was so cool and fresh and she sat so close to me and I was so almost in love with her that I didn't have a single thought of Pamela for at least an entire hour.

And now, all these years later, in the sort-of maid's outfit that Rexall made her wear, Mary filled my coffee cup and watched my face and said, "I just wondered if you'd heard."

"You mean about you and Wes?"

"Umm-hmm."

"Yeah, I did. And congratulations."

"Thanks."

"He's a very nice guy." Actually, he was a nice guy except when it came to me. He didn't like me at all, and I supposed I understood why.

"Yes," she said, "he sure is." Then, "I just decided it was time to have kids, McCain."

She was speaking in a code I understood. What she was really saying was that she was tired of waiting around for me to come to my senses.

"I'm happy for you, Mary. I really am."

She looked as if she was going to say something else but just then two high school girls sat down at the counter. They were best friends. You could tell because they were dressed identically. Poodle haircuts, pink sweaters and large pink skirts decorated with dancing poodles and dancing 45rpm records. The Pink Monster had invaded their brains and taken them over while they slept. The inevitable bobby sox and saddle shoes completed the ensemble. The only thing that kept these two girls from looking like twins was that one was tall and willowy and blonde and the other was short and stout and brunette.

While Mary took their orders for cheeseburgers and fries and Cokes, I wandered over to the magazine stand. Ike was on the cover of *Time* again, responding to the Russian general who'd boasted recently that the USSR had atomic weapons superior to ours. And Dick Nixon was on the cover of *Newsweek* hinting that he just might run for president in 1960. The movie magazines had just come in and were lined neatly in a row, covers featuring Natalie Wood on a motorcycle, Tab Hunter in a cowboy outfit, Brigitte Bardot in a bikini, and Marlon Brando staring somberly out at the world. I picked up *Manhunt*, which had a new Shell Scott story in it, and started back to the counter.

I didn't recognize her at first. I know how odd that sounds. She was, after all, my kid sister, Ruthie, all the years we'd lived in the same house over on Clark Street together, how could I not recognize her? I guess because I always think of Ruthie being happy, but she didn't look happy now. She looked furtive.

She was at the far end of a medicine aisle and it was easy to see what she was doing because she was so bad at it. She was shoplifting. Fortunately for her, there weren't any store employees around. My instinct was to run down the aisle and stop her, but there wasn't time. Her hand flicked out snake-quick, grabbed a small box of some kind, and dumped it in her open purse. Then she started looking frantically around for a way out of the store. She didn't appear to be in danger of becoming a great criminal mastermind.

She started up the aisle and, when she saw me, she froze in place and started looking frantically around again. I walked up to her and slid my arm through hers and whispered, "Why don't you put it back, Ruthie?"

Ruthie got the standard–issue McCain looks. There's a factory somewhere in Indiana, I think, that mass-produces McCains. A family reunion looks like one of those vast General Motors storage lots but instead of hundreds of identical Chevrolets, it's McCains. The outsize blue eyes, the freckles, the slightly imperious nose and the kid-grin. Even Great-grandfather McCain, God love him, looked like he was twenty when he smiled. Even with his store-boughts.

Ruthie wore a black winter coat, open so I could see her black sweater and tight tweed skirt. She had a cute little pink barrette in her short blond hair. She'd bloomed in the past year or so, our little Ruthie, not only pretty but sexy, if I can say that without getting too Freudian. Mom and Dad said our driveway never wanted for junky cars with teenage boys behind the wheels.

"C'mon, Ruthie," I whispered again. "Put it back."

There was panic and embarrassment and anger in her soft blue eyes. I felt all the same things. I didn't want to see my sister get nailed for shoplifting. I also didn't want to see the family name ruined. When I was in tenth grade, we managed to move out of the Knolls and into town, into a nice little frame house. And Dad got a better job, a tie-wearing kind of job, as warehouse manager over at Fugate Industrial, which manufactures safety parts for various kinds of electronic companies. It's not too often Knolls people turn respectable. A shoplifting daughter wouldn't exactly help my folks' reputation. And it wouldn't do a hell of a lot of good for Ruthie, either.

All this was in my head as I tried to grab her arm again without anybody noticing. But as I got to the front of the aisle, Ruthie broke ahead. She nudged into a large display of hula hoops that had been marked down since the summer. But didn't slow down at all. She marched straight to the in-out doors and bolted right out to the sunny street.

I was maybe six steps behind her when I felt a large hand on my shoulder and I turned to see Wes Lindstrom, the pharmacist and the man who was engaged to Mary nodding to my hand. "I hope you're planning to pay for that."

Of course, I first thought of Ruthie. He'd seen her steal the box and wanted restitution. But then he said, "Wouldn't look real good for one of the town's most prominent attorneys to be arrested for shoplifting." And with that he snatched the *Manhunt* magazine from my fingers.

"Oh," I said. "The magazine."

He smiled icily. "It just looks a little suspicious when you're walking out the door with it, without paying for it."

He looked like one of those soap opera actors who play doctors. He was tall with a somewhat craggy face and strawberry-blond hair in a widow's peak. I suppose women found him handsome but there was something superior and judgmental about him. You could see it in his mouth, the way it was always tightening into displeasure and disdain. As it was now.

I dug into my pocket, took out a crumpled dollar bill, and laid it on his palm.

He looked at the magazine cover for the first time. It showed a half-naked woman sprawled on a bloody bed and a dark-suited killer with a gun in his hand crawling out a window.

"Still reading all the intellectual stuff, huh?" His lips became a disapproving editorial on my reading tastes.

"You might like it, if you gave it a try."

"I doubt it. Not with all the medical journals I need to read." He nodded to the sales counter. "I'll get you your change."

I wondered if he really thought I'd been trying to steal the magazine. I wondered also if he'd *tell* people he really thought I'd been trying to steal the magazine. We all like to gossip, I suppose, though of course I'd deny I liked to if you asked me, but Wes was a legendary gossip. He could kill you faster than a bullet. All he had to do was whisper the right words.

He gave me my change then put the magazine in a sack. "People might think you were stealing it otherwise." A quick, icy smile.

"That medicine you gave me for my corns really worked, Wes," an elderly lady said behind me. "I need some more of it."

"You wouldn't have all those corns, Betsy, if you weren't out all night doing the mambo and the cha-cha-cha," he said.

She giggled and you could hear the girl that remained alive inside her despite her seventy years and it was a nice, pure, inspiring sound. I had to give it to Wes. He could be a charmer when he wanted to.

I went back to the counter. "I think your boyfriend thinks I'm a shoplifter."

Mary was wiping off the counter. I told her what happened. "He's just sensitive about you is all. You know, about how you and I grew up together and all."

I wanted to kiss her. Right then and there. I guess it was her

sweetness. Her goodness. I needed something to believe in after
I'd seen my sister stealing that small box.

I spent the next few minutes listening to the radio that played
over the speakers in the store. Small-town radio alternates between Bing Crosby records and local news and what they call
Trader Tom, who conducts a five-minute show every hour to tell
the good people what kind of deal you can get on certain second-
hand items, and who to call if you're interested. Right now, he
was listing a refrigerator, a sectional couch that made into a bed
and a complete collection of *Saturday Evening Post*s from 1941
through the present. I figured my dad would like them. He loved
the western serials, the Ernest Haycox ones especially. Then
Trader Tom had his "Farm Folks" segment where he talked about
the kind of things farmers had up for sale or trade. Today a
farmer had a calf he wanted to trade for a good hunting rifle.
Trader Tom gave the guy's phone number, of course. Townsfolks
always feel superior when they hear the "Farm Folks" segments.
We live in the big city, after all.

Mary came over with the coffeepot but I put my hand over my
cup. "I'm starting to get the jitters."

"You hear about the skating party tonight?"

"Uh-uh."

"They're going to dedicate it to Buddy Holly and Richie Valens
and the Big Bopper and play all the records tonight."

"That's nice."

"I'll probably go if Wes'll let me."

"You have to check with him now?"

She shrugged. "He just thinks it looks funny if I go places
without him. You know, like I'm still single or something."

What the hell are you marrying him for? I wanted to say.
You're so damned decent and smart. And he's such a sanctimo-
nious prig.

But, of course, I didn't say anything like that. I just said, "Well,
maybe I'll check it out."

The phone rang and she excused herself to go get it. I noticed
how her expression changed from a neutral hello to something

more complicated and less friendly. "Just a minute please." She
held the phone out to me. "It's Pamela."

"Oh." I got up and walked down the counter to where the wall
phone was. I walked behind the counter and took the receiver
from her hand.

"I don't think she likes me much," Pamela said. "I suppose it's
because of you."

"So what's going on in the august Judge Whitney's office?" I
said, smiling at Mary as I spoke.

"A lot, actually. She wants you over here right away. Robert
Frazier is in her chambers."

Frazier was the father of Susan, the woman Kenny Whitney
had married. And perhaps murdered.

"I tried to call her honor several times this morning," I said.
"The line was always busy."

"It was crazy here. The press and all. I mean, *both* of them, the
newspaper guy and the radio guy. And it was questions, questions, questions all morning. Finally, Judge Whitney threatened
to get an injunction."

I could see the judge up against the shambling, dandruff-laden
Earle Peterson of *The Bugle* and the crew-cutted nitwit ("Hey,
hang loose, Jack, elsewise I'll be blastin' off, you dig?") Charlie
O'Brian of TOPS radio. Not many people knew this—it was sort
of like the secret identity of the Shadow—but ace reporter and
resident hipster Charlie O'Brian was also the voice of Trader
Tom.

"Well, I'm glad things've calmed down."

"So should I tell her you'll be here right away?"

"Sure. See you."

I hung up and when I turned back to Mary, I felt something I
would've thought impossible. I felt jealous. Wes Lindstrom had
his arm around Mary's shoulder and was talking to her in the
intimate whispers only lovers can understand. And she was smiling up at him, nodding.

When he saw me hang up, he said, loud enough not only for
Mary but for the customers along the counter to hear: "I thought

I had a shoplifter on my hands this morning. Our esteemed counselor here was walking out with a trashy magazine and he acted
surprised when I asked him to pay for it. But I went along with it
and just let him pretend that he'd just forgotten about paying for
it."

There was an angry undertone in his voice and the customers
picked up on it. They weren't sure if they should laugh or not. I
saw Mary watching me, unhappy that he was doing this. I had a
good comeback, even, asking him what he was selling trashy
magazines for in the first place. But I decided against it. The
customers were looking me over now and I could sense that the
tide was against me.

"I'll see you, Mary," I said. I knew I was blushing. I felt alone,
hunted, on the run. Growing up in the Knolls can do that to you.

Life is like that sometimes, as my father always says.

As I was walking out of the store, I slowed down in the aisle
Ruthie had been in. There was a one-box hole in a span of six
small boxes on the shelf. The product was called Potassium
Permangatel. I wondered why she'd want something like that.

SEVEN

THE DAY WAS A postcard, the warm sunlight on the snowy streets making the downtown area look not old but fashionably antique, from the stone gargoyles that guard the entrance to the First National Bank to the octagonal bandstand in the city square where Iowa boy Meredith Wilson of *Music Man* fame had guest-conducted the local symphony three years ago to the three blocks of retail stores, all showing the blue and tan awnings the chamber of commerce had talked them into buying a few years back. The temperature was up around thirty now and the air smelled clean. The people looked clean, too—young, old, rich, poor, clean and bright and friendly, even the young ones in the black leather jackets and the duck's ass haircuts. They liked to play at being bad, some of the older boys, but mostly what they did was cruise the loop area with their radios up too loud and call out to the pretty girls on the streets, and snarl at any male who wasn't dressed the way they were.

There was a shortcut to the courthouse and I took it, down two alleys and one block over. Halfway there, I came out on a narrow side street with a lumberyard, a Western Auto and a small tavern at the very end of the street. It was from the tavern I heard the shout, "You try'n come in here one more time you black bastard, and I'll call the law on you! You see if I don't!"

There was no mistaking the subject of this tirade: Darin Greene. He stood out in front of Paddy's Tap with his hands on his hips, facing down Paddy, who owned the place, and Paddy, Jr., who spent most of his time guzzling up the profits and sounding off on politics. In his cups, he'd tell you that he had some kind of connection to the KKK, but with Paddy, Jr., truth and lies sounded just the same.

Whenever he got drunk and wanted to pick a fight with somebody white, Darin Greene headed for Paddy's, the only tavern in town that wouldn't serve Negroes. Darin had been Kenny Whitney's best friend all the way through school and until a year or so ago when they'd had a mysterious falling-out. In another time, Darin could have been a movie star. He had Harry Belafonte good looks and when he was sober, he could be a charmer. He'd probably had a dozen jobs since high school, losing all of them because of his drinking. He and Kenny had been the football stars. Darin played two years at the University of Iowa but got in trouble busting up a white dean's son in a barroom one hot July night. He served six months in county and then headed straight to Chicago. Nobody saw him for nearly a year and then one day he drove back into town in a shiny new Olds convertible, a fine high-gloss yellow one. He'd lost twenty pounds and looked meaner than ever. The small knife scar he'd picked up on his left cheek didn't hurt, either. Nobody was ever sure how he'd gotten the Olds or the scar but there was a lot of speculation. He immediately started hanging around Kenny again, spending a lot of time out at Kenny's house, and less and less time with his wife and young son, who had not accompanied him to Chicago, Lurlene staying here and working as a nurse's aide at the hospital. Cliff Sykes, Jr., our esteemed police chief, tried for a year to run Darin out of town, but thanks to Judge Whitney, he failed. Judge Whitney wasn't all that crazy about colored people. She just enjoyed thwarting the will of any Sykes anytime she got the chance.

Now, on a beautiful day like this one, two low-life white men were in Darin's face and he was probably too drunk and confused to understand what was going on. He seemed to come to Paddy's on autopilot. He got some kind of terrible pleasure out of it, as if this was the way he secretly believed he *should* be treated.

I walked on over.

Darin was drunker than I thought, weaving back and forth, leaning on the fender of his yellow Olds to keep himself from falling down into the slushy street.

"Why don't you get in your car, Darin?" I said. "I'll call Lurlene and she can come and get you."

"You get your ass out of here, McCain," Paddy, Sr., said. "This buck wouldn't be here if that judge of yours hadn't got all them court orders against Cliff Sykes."

" 'Bout time we started handling things our way," Paddy, Jr., said. "The way they handle 'em down in Mississippi and Alabama."

" 'Til the Jews went down there and started stirring up the coons, anyway," Paddy, Sr., said. Darin was six-three and probably weighed 180 or 190, so it was quite a swing. He'd have shattered Paddy, Sr.'s jaw if the punch had connected. But Darin was off-balance when he threw it and he also slipped on the ice. He followed his punch, ending up on one knee.

Paddy, Jr., moved quickly, raising his foot, ready to catch Darin a good one in the face or chest. Paddy, like his father, was round, sloppy and had a face made for sneering. My rage was right there waiting for me. I supposed Paddy, Jr., could take me in a prolonged fight, but my small size worked for me here. I was faster than he was.

I took the leg he was just about to use on Darin and yanked it out from under him. He sat down on the ice, shocked, enraged and humiliated. He was wearing a new pair of cowboy boots, a new western shirt with fancy piping and a new white Stetson, pretty much the same thing he and his father always wore.

Paddy, Jr., called me a lot of names in a very short time. His father came over and started helping him up. By this time, a number of customers had started wandering out of the small dirty-brick tavern. This was like an extra session of the professional wrestling they watched every Friday night down at the armory. And this was free.

Darin couldn't even get to his feet. I walked over and got one of my arms under one of his and proceeded to inflict a hernia on myself. Somehow I got him to his feet and inside the car. He kept muttering things that I didn't understand at all. I told him, "Get over on the passenger side."

"I can drive, man."

"Sure, you can, Darin. Now get your ass over there."

"I'd watch that white mouth of yours, man."

"Just slide the hell over."

Paddy Hanratty, Sr., was smiling. "He's all yours, McCain. How you like bein' a chauffeur for a coon? Isn't it usually the other way around?"

All the customers standing around found this wonderfully hilarious. They were nudging each other in ludicrous exaggerated ways.

The only one not smiling was Paddy Hanratty, Jr. I'd messed up his cowboy outfit and he was mad. "This isn't over by a long shot, McCain."

I got the key in the ignition. The car barely started. The fine yellow Olds Darin had driven into town a few years ago had now deteriorated just as much as its owner. It hadn't been tuned up for a long time. The windshield was cracked. The floorboards were muddy. Empty beer cans littered the backseat. A Chicago Bears brochure was angrily mashed up in a corner. It was four years old, dating from about the time Darin had tried out for the pros. He was great high school material, solid college material, but no material at all for the pros. Those guys brunch on iron bars.

I got the motor running, albeit raggedly, and then pulled away from the curb. A forest of middle fingers poked the February air at us.

Darin sat up. "I coulda handled that cracker with a gun if I needed to."

"Yeah, you were doing a great job, the way you slipped and fell down."

He glared at me. "You better watch that white mouth of yours." Then, "And anyway, you be drivin' *my* car, asshole, so I'd keep that tongue of yours real civil."

There wasn't any point in arguing with him. He was speaking gibberish way most drunks eventually do. Being near clinical death—his usual alcoholic intake was enormous—he should have passed out. But he just kept right on going. That was the kind of drunk both he and his pal Kenny had been. If they'd gone through everything alcoholic in the house, they'd go into the bathroom and start on the hair tonic that was 14.2 percent alcohol.

We went two blocks and then he muttered something.

"What?" I said.

"Pull the car over!" he screamed at me.

I whipped to the curb. Even before I had the car stopped, he had the door open and was vomiting into the gutter. A couple of lawyers were walking by. They looked pretty disgusted. Then they saw who was driving the Olds and they smirked. There'd be all kinds of jokes about the kind of clientele I had.

He puked for quite a while. He was pretty good at it. He'd puke and then raise his head a little and then puke some more. Then he'd spit. He was almost as good at spitting as puking. I was glad that my next meal was still several hours away.

When he was done, he leaned back inside and said, "Gimme a smoke."

"Yes sir, commander."

I gave him a Pall Mall.

"Light," he said.

I took out the nice silver Ronson my folks had given me for Christmas. I'd already lost it twice but luckily it had kept turning up.

"How much your lighter cost, man?" he said.

"It was a gift."

"Lady friend?"

"My folks. Look, Darin, I have to get going. But there's something I need to do first."

"I coulda handled those two crackers, man."

"When you were sober, yes. Not as drunk as you are now."

"I sound drunk, McCain?"

Actually, he didn't. He sounded, in fact, almost cold sober.

"It's the puking," he said. "It never fails. I just puke my guts up and I'm fine."

"Well, you can never underestimate the medical benefits of puking."

"Straighten me right up. That's how I can last thirty, forty hours drinkin'. I just puke every once in a while."

I started driving again. I pulled into a DX station.

"What you doin'?"

"I need to make a phone call."

I jerked the keys out of the ignition.

"Hey," he said.

"I'll be right back."

"Where you goin' with my keys?"

"I told you. To make a phone call."

"How do I know you ain't gonna try and sell this car or some shit like that?"

"Oh, yeah. I could probably get twenty, thirty grand for this baby. I think the stale beer smell in the backseat is what folks are looking for in a car these days. Not to mention the puke."

"There's that white mouth of yours again."

"Just shut up and sit there, Darin. You're almost as big a pain in the ass as Paddy, Jr."

That quieted him down for some reason.

The pay phone was next to the john. I looked up the hospital number and called. I asked for Lurlene and the operator said just a minute. Out in the car repair section, the greasy silver hoist was raising up a very cherry 1953 DeSoto. A kid in a clean DX uniform was using his wrench to point out various things on the undercarriage of a car. I was getting sentimental. Nothing I'd rather do than spend a warm afternoon on my driveway working on my ragtop.

Lurlene came on and I told her who I was and what had happened.

"Did he throw up?" she asked.

"Yes, as a matter of fact, he did."

"Then he should be all right to drive."

"He may be all right technically. But I'll bet that Sykes still comes after him." I was sure that Paddy, Sr., had called Chief of Police Sykes, and I was sure that Sykes would be waiting for Darin Greene to get behind the wheel. They'd hit him with several charges, including drunken driving and, for sure, resisting arrest, which would justify the beating they would certainly put on him.

"I'm sorry, Mr. McCain, it's just that they don't like me takin' time off at the hospital here. They're real nice and I hate to take advantage. And you know, with Darin not workin', I'm the only support our family's got."

"All right. I'll run him home."

"That's very nice of you, Mr. McCain."

I hesitated, knowing what I was about to say would disturb her. "Does Darin have a gun?"

"A gun? He has a hunting rifle. I bought him one at Sears a couple years ago. For his birthday. Jeff, he's the oldest boy, he's eight, he's startin' to take target practice with it in the Cub Scouts."

"How about a handgun?"

"He's got that Army .45 his daddy had in the war."

That must be the gun he was referring to when I'd gotten into his car.

"Is he in some kind of trouble?"

"Not at all," I said. "He just mentioned it in passing."

Another pause. "Is he in trouble, Mr. McCain?"

"No. He really isn't, Lurlene."

"Would you swear to it on the Lord's name?"

"I swear to it on the Lord's name."

"Oh, thank God. I just got so scared there." She sounded about to cry. "The boys, they're just always afraid somethin' bad's gonna happen to that daddy of theirs." Now she was crying, not hard, but with the soft, earnest sounds of a good and weary woman. "He ain't like people say he is, Mr. McCain, not when he's sober. When he's sober, he can be the nicest man in the world."

When I hung up, I dropped in another nickel and called my dad and asked him if he could meet me out at Darin Greene's place in about twenty minutes. And that I'd explain later.

When I went back out to the Olds, Darin was leaning against the front of the car, one heel hooked on the bumper. He had to be cold in his short-sleeved red shirt and tan slacks. He did not look happy.

When I got close, he held his hand out. "Keys."

"I'm driving you home."

"Keys, man. Or I'm gonna make you very sorry."

I looked at him. He wasn't a bully, as Kenny had been. But he had a much deeper and meaner anger. He could make me very sorry indeed.

"Sykes is going to be laying for you."

"I don't give a damn about Sykes right now, man. I just want my keys back."

"You want your kids to have to come and visit you in county again?"

That got to him. Say what you would about him, what he was or wasn't, he was a man who loved his kids.

"You son of a bitch."

But he got in the car. The passenger's side.

When we were going again, he reached under the seat and brought up a pint of rotgut whiskey.

"You really need that?"

"You're pushin' your luck, man. And that's no shit."

"I take it you heard about Kenny."

" 'Course I heard about Kenny. Everybody's heard about Kenny."

"I don't think he killed her."

"What're you talkin' about, man, of course he killed her."

"We'll see."

"If he didn't kill her, why'd he kill himself, then?"

"I was hoping maybe you could help me out a little with that one."

He glowered at me again. He looked angry, as he often did, but now there was a sense of fear about him, too. I wondered what he was afraid of.

We were out on the river road now, heading toward the trailer court where virtually every Negro in the county lived. The rent is cheap, I guess. It's our form of segregation.

"You were his friend, is what I mean. I thought maybe you could help me."

"You haven't kept up. Me 'n' Kenny haven't spoken in over a year."

"Why?"

"None of your business why."

"Friendship like that, all those years, and it just ends. That doesn't make much sense."

"I don't know anything about what happened out there. Far as I can tell, he killed Susan and then he killed himself. He got crazy when he drank and from what I hear, he'd been hittin' it pretty hot 'n' heavy."

We came up on a little hill. On a wide grassy field below were the trailers. They were the small jobs, the kind they'd built before the war. There were maybe three dozen of them. It was a ghetto. Saturday nights, the good colored folks stayed inside all locked up while the predators prowled. I sometimes felt sorry for myself, coming from the Knolls. But what I'd had to put up with was easy compared to the doom that awaited the black kids from Shady Acres Trailer Park.

I found his trailer and pulled up. The yard was picked up and the trailer looked homey with crisp yellow-flowered curtains in the windows.

He looked over at me and grinned coldly. "You went to all this trouble, man, and I wasn't no help at all, was I?"

"Nope. You weren't."

"And I ain't gonna be, either."

I decided to lay it out for him. "I'll be real interested in what caliber gun killed Susan Whitney."

The fear was in his face again. "It ain't none of my business, man. And I could care less about them two."

I left the keys in the ignition and opened the door. In the rear-view, I could see my dad's blue '52 Chevy coupe coming up the road.

I got out, closed the door, and then leaned back in. "You ever find that forty-five of yours, let me know."

"How'd you know it was a forty-five, man? Huh?"

But I'd decided to be just as uncooperative as he was. "See you around, Darin."

Then I walked back to my dad's coupe.

EIGHT

I STILL REMEMBER STANDING ON the platform at the train depot and watching my dad wave to us when he came home from World War II. I was shocked. My parents are small people. My mom is five-two and has never cleared ninety pounds. But I'd grown up with my mom and was used to her size. My dad was a different matter. I'd seen a lot of John Wayne and Ronald Reagan—two of the many brave movie stars who hadn't actually gone to war—war movies, and so I just figured my dad would be this big heroic kind of guy, too. He'd been gone a long time. Well, he wasn't big and heroic-looking. In fact, he looked like a kid. He was five-six and weighed maybe 130 and had dishwater blond hair. His khaki uniform looked too big for him, gave him a vulnerability that made him seem even less soldierly. He was an utter stranger to me. The last time I'd seen him I'd been seven years old. I felt sort of ashamed of him, actually, how young and vulnerable he looked in the midst of all these other towering GIs. Why couldn't I have a dad who looked like Robert Mitchum? And I've always been ashamed of myself for feeling that. I know that when I see him in his coffin over at the Fitzpatrick Funeral Home, that's what I'll think of, how I betrayed him in my heart that first day he came back from the war.

The other thing I always remember about him was how he used to jitterbug with my mother on the linoleum in the kitchen in those good giddy days right after the fighting stopped. They'd play the Andrews Sisters and Ella Fitzgerald and Benny Goodman and Glenn Miller and they'd dance for hours. But he managed. They stayed home a lot, as if they didn't want to share each other with anybody else. They'd have a quart of Hamms beer on the oilcloth-covered table (I've always loved the smell of oilcloth) and the amber eye of the radio would burn far into the night as music poured from its speakers.

That wasn't too long ago but it was hard to believe it was the same guy. Bald, stooped, nearsighted. The war hadn't taken nearly as much out of him as his various jobs did afterward. Just as I'd barely recognized him that day on the train platform, I had a hard time recognizing him these days. Small to begin with, now he seemed to shrink even smaller in his gray Penney's overcoat and blue Irish wool walking cap.

I got in the car. The heater was on. So was Bill Haley. Somehow my dad had picked up a fondness for rock and roll, one not shared by my mom. He was watching Darin slip and slide up to his trailer.

"I wonder what the hell went wrong with him," my dad said. "I always thought he'd have a nice future. And he's got such a nice wife and all." He shook his head. "I s'pose it's growin' up out here. How colored people get treated, I mean." Dad had all the insecurities that go along with being a small and somewhat delicate man. But instead of using them to hate or bully, he'd turned them into empathy and wisdom. He always watched the *CBS Evening News* with Douglas Edwards and watched what the white cops were doing to black people trying to ride whites-only city buses. Stuff like that got to him as much as it did me. Even my mom, who didn't vote because she hated all politicians equally, had tears in her eyes when she saw little Negro kids blasted off the streets with fire hoses and their parents clubbed to their knees.

"I found him over at Paddy's."

Dad made a face. "I wonder why he does that. He knows they'll just throw him out. Poor bastard."

He put the coupe in reverse, we whipped backward into a small drive, and then turned back toward town. The coupe was warm and snug.

"Sykes is lookin' for you."

"Sykes?" I said.

"Yeah. He called the warehouse and asked if I knew where you were. And then he called your mom out to the house."

"He say what he wanted?"

"Said you shouldn't have left Kenny Whitney's house before he told you to. He said he could arrest you for leaving. What a dip-shit that guy is. I had a captain like him in the army. Always struttin' around and actin' like he was on top of things. Drove a truck straight off a mountainside when were in Italy. Luckily, he was the only one who died."

"Well, I'm going to see Judge Whitney first. That's been my plan all day but I can't get in, she's so damned busy."

He looked at me, this old man who had yet to see his fiftieth birthday. "She been any nicer to you lately?"

I smiled. "Not so's you'd notice."

"Well, I don't have to tell you how the Whitneys are."

"Eastern money," I said. "*Big* Eastern money. The only thing I could never figure out is why her branch moved clear the hell out here to Iowa."

We were passing a supermarket on the edge of town. Dad read some of the prices in the windows out loud. "Gosh, look. Pork steak is thirty-three cents a pound. And bacon is three for a buck. Guy'd have to be a millionaire if he wanted to eat a good steak these days." As a child of the Depression, Dad watched food prices the way other men watched stock prices. Overseas and dreaming of home, the men of his generation had imagined heaven on earth when they returned home. They hadn't known that heaven had inflation and bad spells of recession, too. "You know Ross, the guy I work with? You know what he paid for his new Mercury? Three thousand dollars. Hell, we paid that for the *house* when we bought it."

"You were going to tell me why the Whitneys came out here."

"Oh. I forgot. The Whitneys. Well, the judge's grandfather got caught in a land swindle, one of those deals that's so complicated it gives you a headache to think about. Anyway, what it came down to was that her grandfather cheated the government and they were going to bring him to trial and everything, but the family chipped in and gave the cash back and got the government to drop the charges. And then they gave him a lot of money and told him to get lost somewhere on the frontier. Iowa was as far as he got."

I laughed. "So that story she hands out about her grandfather coming out here because he wanted to be a gentleman farmer—"

"A total crock."

We were in town and headed toward the one-story corner brick building where I have my office around back. Dad pulled into the parking lot and said, "Mom wants to know when you're coming over for dinner."

"How about next Tuesday?"

"Spaghetti night. She makes the best."

Mom did housework with military-style orderliness. For years, Tuesday night had been spaghetti night just as Tuesday day had been housecleaning day, just as Wednesday was Swiss steak night and grocery shopping day. She did all these things on a budget so minuscule I felt like a spendthrift every time I bought a candy bar.

Dad said, "You didn't mention Kenny."

I looked over at him. "I don't think he killed her."

"That isn't what I was thinkin' of."

"Oh?"

"I was thinkin' of how he was always beating you up. Ever since you were in kindergarten together. And I could never protect you and I felt like hell about it. I remember the time he broke your glasses and I drove out to their mansion and I was ready to be all pissed and everything but when I got inside there I was really intimidated. The way they looked at me and talked to me.

It should've made me even madder. But it just kind of beat me down. I shoulda stuck up for you a lot better, but I didn't. All he did, Kenny's old man, was scratch out this check and hand it to me and tell me to never come out there again. I felt ashamed of myself, I really did, kiddo. I really did."

I put my hand on his shoulder. "You did the best you could, Dad. I wouldn't have done any better."

Then he circled back. "So how come you don't think he killed her?"

"I'm not sure. Just a feeling, I guess."

He thought a moment and said, "You know what I shoulda done the day I was out at their mansion?"

"What?"

"I had real muddy shoes on. I took them off at the door. I shoulda tracked mud all the way into his den."

I laughed at the picture of my small father leaving big mud prints on the mansion floor. It was like watching a really funny *Daffy Duck* cartoon.

"Well, kiddo," he said, glancing at his Timex. "I better head back."

I watched him pull away, and then I walked over to the imperious Judge Whitney's chambers, the same Judge Whitney whose grandfather had been a federal land swindler.

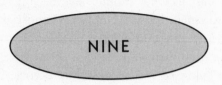

NINE

T HE STONE COURTHOUSE HAD been built before there were any Whitneys *or* Sykeses to fight over who would get the building contract. It was three stories high, with a small golden dome that flew the American flag, and had the feel of an Italian Renaissance castle in an MGM musical with Mario Lanza and Kathryn Grayson. For my taste, it was too fancy by half. Cliff Sykes, Sr., was always hinting he'd like to tear it down and build a new one. He'd go to the opposite extreme. The one he'd build would look like the prefab home developments he was putting up on both ends of town.

Judge Whitney's chambers were on the second floor. I'd missed the rush. The outer office, which was nicely carpeted wall-to-wall and filled with mahogany furnishings and several large portraits of Whitney menfolk down the decades, was empty. There was an American flag standing in the corner and a portrait of George Washington on the wall next to it. Empty like this, and with paintings of all these dead people, there was a hushed, churchlike air about the place.

The air was soon changed by a beautiful face and a beautiful body, namely one Pamela Forrest. She walked through the door with an aluminum coffeepot in her hand. "Want some?"

"Please."

"The judge has extra cups in there."

She wore a white turtleneck sweater and a blue jumper. She looked very smart in what should have been a fairly humdrum outfit. She also smelled great. I always wondered if I wasn't in love with her perfumes and not her at all.

"Is Frazier still in there?"

She made a face. She was speaking sotto voce. "He's very upset."

"His daughter's dead. I don't blame him."

"He seems to be holding the poor judge responsible for everything Kenny ever did."

Over the years, the Eastern Whitneys shipped most of their ne'er-do-wells out here to Iowa. Kenny's father had been a womanizer. He went through three wives and numerous affairs before he finally cracked his car up on Hopkins Road one night. Needless to say, he'd also been a drinker. The Eastern branch of the family had sent him out here originally because he'd plundered a trust fund that was to be used for philanthropy. He ended up routing a lot of the money to some of his European cronies, who sported such dubious titles as prince, duke and viceroy. When the trust fund was nearly depleted, the family put Kenny's father and Kenny on a plane and dispatched them out here, where the father was to oversee the family's rather large cattle holdings. He was smart enough to hire a good manager, a former rodeo star whose baptismal name was Tex (presumably after the well-known Saint Tex), and spend the rest of his time chasing ladies. Without a mother—Mom having run off with one of those titled fellows of dubious cachet—Kenny had only his father to raise him, which went a long way to explaining why Kenny had turned out as he had. Kenny's father had been the drunken twit who'd tossed my dad out of the family manse.

I followed Pamela into the judge's chambers.

Before I'd even crossed the threshold, two familiar scents obliterated Pamela's perfume, the odors of Gauloise cigarettes—yes, the ones in the blue packages French people always smoke while they're talking in subtitles after having sex—and Eiffel Tower brandy. Except for when she's in court, you seldom see the judge without a Gauloise and a snifter of brandy on her desk.

Esme Anne Whitney was born in New York City a decade or so before the turn of the century. She'd been schooled abroad for the most part—London, Paris, Rome—all before she was fifteen, when her parents died in a train accident. She was then sent out here to live with her oldest brother, a fairly decent guy as Whitneys go, an honest politician and a man who seemed to have some genuine concern for those less lucky than himself. He ended up as a judge and influenced Esme to attend law school at the University of Iowa. She would have preferred Yale or Harvard but her brother had taken sick and she wanted to be around him. Three years out of law school, she used her influence with then President Coolidge to get herself appointed to her ailing brother's seat on the bench. She has been there ever since.

She's an elegant woman. She buys all her clothes in New York and it shows. She's slender to the point of emaciation, Roman-esque in the brazen jut of nose and the impudence of eyes and upper lip. Her head would look great in profile stamped on a silver coin. She wears her graying hair cropped close and only enough makeup to lend drama to her already dramatic features. Her speech is as eccentric as her Gauloises, a touch of Kate Hepburn, a dollop of Ayn Rand, whose books fill the glass book-case behind her massive leather executive chair.

This afternoon, she wore a gray fitted suit, gray hose and black pumps. She had nice legs. She was propped on the edge of her vast desk, the smoke in one hand, the brandy in the other.

She was speaking to an austere man with white hair and a bad complexion. He wore a blue blazer, white shirt, regimental striped tie, gray slacks. On his blazer pocket was a fancy crest. Bob Frazier was the only man in the county Judge Whitney would even consider a social peer. Though he was local money— his father having owned outright as many as four short-line rail-roads at one time—he'd spent most of his school years in London, ending up at Oxford. I probably would have felt sorrier for him if he hadn't left his daughter alone for months at a time when she was a young girl. She'd always been a nice kid, but she had a desperate edge. You get that way when you don't have a parent in your life.

"Bob, for God's sake," the judge was saying, "if you want me to say that my nephew, Kenny, was a shit, *of course* he was a shit. You don't really expect me to sit here and deny that, do you? But beyond admitting it, what else can I do about it? I'm sorry; I'm very, very sorry it happened."

"Excuse me," Pamela said before Frazier could respond. "I brought some more coffee. Fresh."

"Thank you, dear," the judge said. "So pour us some fresh and get the hell out of here."

"Yes, Judge."

To me, she said, "You're late."

I didn't have time to say anything. I just sat down in the leather chair next to Frazier's. He briefly scowled in my direction. I'd never liked him but now that his daughter was dead, I felt vaguely guilty about not liking him. While Pamela poured everybody coffee, I sat there and tried hard to work up some good feelings for him. I didn't have much luck.

"Now, you have some brandy in this one, Bob," the judge said. Pamela had handed her a cup and saucer. The judge picked up the brandy bottle and poured in a good shot and handed the cup to Bob. The judge dispensed brandy-and-coffee the way priests dispensed communion.

"It's too early," Frazier said.

"The hell if it is," the judge said. "Now hold your cup out and quit being a baby."

"Damn it, Esme, there's never any arguing with you, is there?" Frazier said, but he held his cup out. The judge gave him a bracing shot. No matter how strong your resolve was, the judge would triumph.

"What you need to do," the judge said, "as soon as the funeral is over is get the hell out of here. And I mean far away. Have you ever been to Bermuda?"

"Once. They were having some kind of political trouble there. And some kind of big bug bit my girlfriend on the ass. Pardon my French."

"Which girlfriend?"

"Darla."

"Did the bug get poisoned?" the judge asked sweetly.

"She never liked you any better than you liked her," Frazier said. Then he made a fist. And his eyes shone with tears. "My daughter was a good, sweet girl and that son of a bitch completely corrupted her. Completely."

On the words "good, sweet girl," the judge looked at me and rolled her eyes. His daughter, Susan, whom I'd liked, probably hadn't been an ideal girl. She slept around a lot and had a few minor fracases with Sykes' hillbilly gestapo. But she was a sweet and tender and honest girl, giving a lot of free hours to the hospital and to one of the local vets. She was like a lot of local people, she saw helping out as part of the price you paid for the privilege of living here.

Frazier suddenly set his cup down and half-leaped to his feet. He walked over to the regal red drapes keeping out the afternoon sun. He parted the drapes and looked out. The sun exposed the rough acne of his face. Mid-fifties, and his complexion had never cleared up. But somehow, with the white hair and the sharply pointed nose, the affliction only enhanced his predatory air.

Still staring out the window, he said, "She was my life. She was all I cared about."

The judge gave me another one of her skeptical looks but let him go on.

He turned back to look at her. "I don't have to tell you that I was opposed to this marriage."

"Oh, don't worry, Bob. I remember how much you were against it."

"Kenny was a jackass."

"That he was."

"And the idea that he'd run around on a young woman as beautiful and gentle as my daughter—" He shook his white-maned head and for the first time I felt sorry for him. I wondered now if he was reliving everything his mother had put his father through. Her affairs were the stuff of local legend. She'd been the artsy-type, involved in theater productions and arts festivals and outdoor musicales, as they are called. She'd spent a good deal of her time at a downtown store called Leopold Bloom's, after the James Joyce character. She was his first wife and no one could blame him for finally divorcing her. But then he pretty much married the same woman three times over.

Frazier came back to his chair. He looked old and weak now. The sunlight had apparently put him in a better mood. He said, "You're right, Esme. I want to punish somebody. It's just like Kenny to kill himself. The bastard couldn't face what he'd done, so he took the easy way out."

"I don't think he killed her," I said.

They both looked at me.

"What the hell're you talking about?" Frazier said.

I glanced at the judge. "I don't think he killed her. I don't know why I say that—it's just an instinct, I guess. He was so drunk, he *thought* he *might* have killed her. But I think somebody else was there with them right before I came."

"And of course you don't have any idea who?" he said.

"Not yet, I don't."

"I can't think straight," he said to the judge. "I don't even know what the hell he's talking about."

"Neither do I, Bob," she said, sounding peeved as only the judge can sound peeved. "But believe me, I'm going to find out."

He gathered up his camel hair coat from the coatrack. "There's a lot of things I need to do this afternoon."

"I'll be here or at home if you need me," the judge said.

"You're a true friend, Esme. And I appreciate it."

He slipped into his coat. I still didn't like him and I probably never would. It was pretty obvious the feeling was mutual. "As for you, McCain, I'd keep your mouth shut unless you have some evidence in hand."

The hell of it was, he was right. I shouldn't have said anything about my theory unless I had something to support it.

He walked to the door. He looked lost again suddenly. "Thanks, Esme."

"You're most welcome, Bob."

When he was gone, she lit up a Gauloise and said, "So tell me, McCain, how're you going to save that prick's reputation?"

"What?"

"Kenny," she said impatiently. "I don't mind that he killed himself. Given the way that he'd screwed up his life, that was almost a noble act. But to kill poor Susan—tell me why you don't think he did it."

I shook my head. "Frazier was right. I shouldn't have said anything."

"Frazier's a windbag," she said. "He's just worried that by the time Sykes gets done rummaging through Susan's life, the whole Frazier family will have another scandal on their hands. You know, the way he did with his first wife. Susan was definitely a tramp."

"She was actually a decent kid," I said.

"Here we go," she said, blew smoke aimed at me. "McCain riding to the defense of the poor damsel."

"She ran around," I said. "But she had good reason to. Kenny lost interest in her a long time ago."

"Don't put me in a position of having to defend Kenny," she said, "because that's impossible. But she could have always left him, broken it off clean."

"She loved him."

"So she slept around on him?"

"People do strange things when they're hurt," I said. "I think we have to keep that in mind. I knew her for a long time. She was sweet and very decent."

The judge smiled coldly. "Does that mean you slept with her?"

"We went out a few times before she married Kenny."

"That doesn't answer my question."

"I know. I don't *intend* to answer your question."

She laughed. "Ah. Stand up to me. I like that. Sometimes."

"I just don't want to hear her rundown. She doesn't deserve it."

"Spare me, McCain," she said, pouring more coffee into her brandy. After taking a sip, she said, "Fifteen minutes ago I thought I'd have to call my father in New York and tell him that someone in our family had committed murder. Believe me, I wasn't looking forward to it. That would look very bad on the family résumé, as it were. But you, you McCain, have given me new hope. Maybe Kenny didn't kill her at all."

She looked happy. Two people were dead and she looked happy. This was one of those moments I resented being her minion. This had all become an elitist game to her. One could abide a suicide in one's family if one had to. But murder was another matter. No matter how far back it was stuffed into the family closet, somebody was always dragging it out of the cold, damp shadows.

"Now what you need to do, McCain," she said, "is prove it. Because you know what's going to happen here. Sykes is going to say it was a murder-suicide and close the books on it."

"You're probably right."

"Probably? Probably? My God, McCain, you've known that moron as long as I have. He'll have this whole thing wrapped up by sundown. If he hasn't already. So get busy."

I stood up. I'd been thinking about going to the tribute skating party for Buddy Holly tonight. Didn't sound as if I was going to have time.

"It was probably one of her lovers," the judge said. "He probably snuck in there and shot her and Kenny was so drunk he couldn't remember it."

I got into my topcoat. "I have to warn you about something."

"What?"

"I could be wrong."

"You mean that Kenny might actually have killed her?"

"Yes."

"Well, you sure as hell'd better *not* be wrong."

"I figured you would probably say something like that."

"Listen, McCain. You were the one who brought this up. Now hustle your ass out there and get to work."

I nodded.

Then she raised her right hand and shot me.

Just once I didn't want to jerk when the rubber band came at me. But for some reason, I always did.

"You flinched!" she said. She sounded like a kid, albeit a kid with a brandy- and Gauloise-ravaged voice. She strung another rubber band across her thumb and forefinger. "Care to try for two out of three?"

"Why don't you let me try that once on you?" I said.

"Well, of course not. I'm a lady."

"Ah."

"And I'm also your boss. Now get going, McCain. My family's honor is at stake here."

Yes, I thought, I certainly wouldn't want to besmirch the good name of a family that included Kenny and the judge's great-grandfather, the land swindler.

I left the office.

Pamela was typing. "Poor Mr. Frazier."

"I hate to say this. But he's a jerk. She deserved a lot better father and a lot better husband." I leaned to her desk. "If I can get free tonight, how about going to the skating party with me?"

"I'm hoping to see Stu there, actually."

"You have a date with him?"

"Not a date exactly but—"

I couldn't help it. I had to say it. At this moment, I just plain felt sorry for her and needed to give her brotherly advice. "You're just going to show up, huh, and hope he shows up, too, huh?"

She blushed. "Well. . ."

"How long are you going to chase after him, anyway?"

But she was ready for that one "How long are you going to chase after me, McCain? If we were sensible, I'd be in love with you and you'd be in love with Mary. But here we are."

"Yes," I said. "Here, we are."

TEN

OUR WEST SIDE A & W Root Beer stand is what you might call indomitable. It stays open year-round. In the summer you're served by cute girls in black short-shorts and white blouses and great tanned legs. Some of them even skate your cheese-burger and fries out to you. There are a few mishaps, of course, not all the girls being championship roller skaters. My sister, Ruthie, was a carhop for two summers and set the record for falling in love, her two-month summer gig resulting in 4,321 in-fatuations and 3,964 Real Things. And there's always rock and roll on the speakers, much to the dismay of some of the older citizens, though you have to wonder what they're doing here in the first place. Bill Haley, Eddie Cochran, Ricky Nelson, the Plat-ters, Frankie Avalon, all the greats and sort-of greats help you digest the wonderfully greasy food. And day or night, there's summer promise in the air, swimming and beer at the sandpits, drag racing and beer out on the highways, making out and beer in a myriad of backseats.

Winter is a different matter. The girls come out all bundled up in parkas and gloves and there's no flirting, either. It's too cold to flirt. They just hand you your order through the window and disappear back inside, their breath silver on the prairie winter air.

Today was no different.

The last food I'd had was a doughnut on my way back from Kenny Whitney's. Now I sat at the A&W listening to the Paul Anka sob "Lonely Boy." Even the music was more subdued in the winter, Paul Anka being a long way from Fats Domino.

I was just finishing up when I saw Debbie Lundigan walking on the sidewalk past the A&W. She'd been a good friend of Susan Whitney. I stuffed the remains of my early dinner into the paper bag, backed up until I reached the large wire wastebasket, put it straight in the basket for two points and then backed up and wheeled around so I could reach the exit drive just as Debbie was about to cross it.

I rolled down my window and said, "Hi, Debbie. You like a ride?"

"Oh, hi, McCain. I'm just walking over to Randy's." Randy's was the supermarket used by most people on this side of town, which was mostly a working-class neighborhood.

"Get in. I'm going right by there."

When she got inside, I could see she'd been crying. She was a tall and somewhat awkward woman. We'd gone to school together since kindergarten. She had one of those wan faces that is pretty in an almost oppressive way. She always looks as if she might break into tears at any moment. She'd gotten married three weeks after we graduated from high school. It had always been a rocky marriage made even rockier by Susan Whitney. They'd gone to school together for years but had never paid much attention to each other. Suddenly, they were fast friends, two married women with bad marriages. Debbie's husband had taken to hitting her; Susan's to ignoring her. There was a lot of town talk about them being easy lays after a few drinks but you couldn't prove it by me. I've never had any luck at all with women who are called easy. In fact, once I hear a woman described that way, I know I'll never score, not even with a sub-machine gun and a bag of cash. Life is like that sometimes.

Debbie wore a pair of festive red earmuffs and a winter jacket with a fake-fur collar, jeans and loafers with bobby sox. Her nose was red from the cold and looked little-girl sweet. She took a pack of Winstons from her jacket pocket and tamped one out on her gloved hand. She pushed in my car lighter and when it popped out, got her weed going.

She said, after exhaling, "I just hope this town is sorry now for the way they treated her. You know, like she was some whore or something."

I didn't have to ask who she was talking about.

"She was the nicest girlfriend I ever had. You know how many clothes she bought me? Like this jacket for instance. You know how much she paid for it? Thirty-nine dollars. And you know why? Because she said she was tired of seeing me freeze all the time. She knew I couldn't afford one like this. Thirty-nine dollars. So I hope all those bastards are happy now that she's finally dead."

"I don't think he killed her."

She looked stunned. Or stricken. I wasn't sure which. "What? Chief Sykes is *telling* everybody he killed her." That was the nice thing about a small town. You didn't have to worry about your pronouns. We hadn't mentioned any names but we knew exactly whom we were talking about.

"You really believe anything Chief Sykes has to say?"

"Then who killed her, McCain?"

"That's what I need to find out. I thought maybe you could tell me who she was hanging around with lately. Guys, I mean."

"Nobody in particular."

The late-afternoon traffic was starting to pile up, our version of rush hour. The shadows were starting to kidnap the day, the sky layered salmon and gold and a kind of celestial puce. Kids were lobbing snowballs back and forth, yard to yard. Scarves were trailing behind the prone bodies of kids steering their sleds down-hill to the sidewalks. In a lot of houses, small groups of kids would be gathered in front of the TV watching *Hopalong Cassidy* or *Howdy Doody* or the *Three Stooges*. And moms in kitchens would be starting supper, the smells rich and good on the chill melancholy of the fading winter day, spaghetti and pot roasts and cheese casseroles.

"I really need you to think hard, Debbie."

"I knew that's what you wanted."

"What I wanted?"

"Yeah, when you pulled up back there. That you wanted to talk to me about Susan."

"You were her best friend."

She took another drag and looked out the window. "I really like this town."

"So do I."

"I just wish people didn't gossip so much."

"It's just the way people are. And most people here *don't* gossip that much. Just a few of them. And it doesn't matter where you move to because they'll be that way there, too."

"I suppose." Then, "She wasn't screwing a lot of guys, if that's what you mean."

"I didn't say she was."

"She only slept with a couple of guys."

"I don't suppose you'd tell me who they are."

"I wasn't screwing a lot of guys, either."

"I'm sure you weren't." Then, "Would you tell me who she was sleeping with?"

"Well, Tommy Fennelly for one. But he left for the service three months ago. Camp Pendleton."

"Wasn't he a little young for her?"

"He was nineteen. But he's a real nice kid. A couple of times, he tried to get her off the booze. He sat up with her the whole night at his apartment, she told me. Let her cry and throw up and tear his place apart. She quit for a while, too. Couple of weeks, one time. Not one single drink that whole time."

Tommy Fennelly had always seemed to me nothing much more than a loafer—a little pool, a few card games, minor trouble with the law now and then. But Debbie had swept all that away. She'd just made him a damned nice kid.

"Who else?"

She sighed. "And Steve Renauld."

"At Leopold Bloom's?"

"Yeah. I couldn't believe it, either. He's such a loser. Mr. High and Mighty."

"How the hell did she get hooked up with him?"

"Well, you know, we used to go in there and look around. He and his wife have nice stuff in there. Or anyway that's what Susan told me. I couldn't tell. I mean, Susan was educated. I'm just a bumpkin."

"Same here."

"You're a *lawyer*, McCain."

"A lot of lawyers are bumpkins."

"Really?"

"Hell, yes."

"Well, you're not as much of a bumpkin as *I* am, anyway."

"So you started going to Renauld's place."

"And he started asking Susan if he could paint her. Him and his painting. I used to call him 'Vincent Van Phony.' He heard me once and really got pissed off. But he kind of wore her down. And she started posing for him. You know, he's got that so-called studio over on Jackson Street. That's where they did the dirty deed, anyway."

"When was this?"

"About a month ago. She said they were both pretty drunk the times it happened."

"She tell you anything else?"

"Just that he wasn't much in the sack and that she sort of felt sorry for him. She said that once and I've always remembered it."

"Said what?"

"Said she couldn't sleep with a man she didn't feel sorry for. She didn't like most men. Said they all reminded her of her father. You know, the swaggering type and everything. Renauld's pretty pathetic so I guess that's why she slept with him. But I think she got scared."

"Of what?"

"Of Renauld. He was making it a lot more of it than it was.

She went to bed because she felt sorry for him, like I said. But he saw it as this big romance. He was going to leave his wife and daughter. He wanted them to move to Iowa City. You know, he was always talking like Iowa City was—what's that place the Arabs always go to?"

"Mecca?"

"Yeah, he always talked like Iowa City was Mecca. Or something. She was going to run away from Kenny and he was going to run away from his wife and they were going to be this real cool artistic couple and live in Iowa City."

"And she didn't see it that way?"

"Are you kidding? She got to be as afraid of Renauld as she was of Kenny. He really started putting a lot of pressure on her."

We were at the supermarket. I swung into the drive. A lot of people left their cars running. You could see the exhaust putt-putting out of their mufflers. Folks trust one another out here, and that's nice.

"Maybe you should talk to Renauld," she said, opening the door and flipping the butt of her Winston out the door.

"That's a good idea."

"I just hope, if Kenny didn't kill her, you find out who did."

"So do I," I said.

She was gone then, hurrying through the dusk into the lights and hustle of the supermarket where a hundred shoppers were trying to hurry their way home.

ELEVEN

I DROVE PAST THE POLICE station. The big black Indian motorcycle, the one belonging to our esteemed police chief, Cliff Sykes, Jr., wasn't there.

A block away, I pulled up to a phone booth. It was getting dark, cold-winter dark. Across the street was a small diner with a long, wide front window. Edward Hopper was my favorite painter and the window of the diner looked like something he would have painted; there were six, seven working-class men sitting at a long counter eating their dinner but not in any way communicating with anybody else. Totally isolated in this little strip of light in the otherwise black prairie night. Even the plump waitress in the pink uniform, standing alone by the cash register, seemed forever cursed by isolation and loneliness.

I put in my nickel.

"Hello?"

"Were you eating, Mom?"

"No, honey. But I'll be putting supper on the table in about fifteen minutes if you want to come over."

"I'm afraid I'm working tonight."

"For yourself or the judge?"

I lied. "For myself."

"Good. You'll be on your own if you just keep trying. Won't that be nice when you don't have to work for the judge anymore?" Having grown up in the Knolls, my mother had no time for the imperious Whitneys.

"Is Ruthie there, Mom?"

"No, hon. I'm afraid she already left for the library. Said she had a lot of homework to do. School seems to be getting her down this year."

"Oh?"

"She looked so tired lately. And her appetite's awful."

"How's Dad?"

"Well, *Cheyenne* is on tonight so he's happy. You know how he likes his westerns."

The judge had been nice enough to give me a good bonus at Christmastime. I'd finally been able to replace my family's old 12-inch Arvin with a brand-new 21-inch Admiral console. Now Dad could really enjoy his westerns.

"We'd like to see you sometime, hon."

"I know, Mom. It's just I've been so busy."

"Well, the water's boiling over on the potatoes. I'd better grab them. Thanks for calling."

I spent a lot of time in the library when I was a kid. I liked books. But I also liked girls and the library was a good place to sit with a book and watch girls troop in and out. I think even back then, I was looking for a girl to make me forget Pamela. She was never a girl from the Knolls, though. She had to be better than the Knolls. Just as, for Pamela, her ideal man had to be from old, secure money and reputation. Sometimes I wondered if that was the only thing Pamela and I had in common, our shallowness.

On a cold winter night, the steam heat was turned all the way up and the pipes clanked ferociously. The library was built with a Carnegie grant right after the turn of the century. It was still a pleasant place but it was starting to get too small. At dinnertime, the library was largely empty. I couldn't find Ruthie anywhere on the ground floor. I paused long enough to look over the best sellers, from *Majorie Morningstar* by Herman Wouk to *Doctor Zhivago* by Boris Pasternak, *The Robe* by Lloyd C. Douglas. I'd still take John D. MacDonald and Peter Rabe.

I went upstairs, to the reference section. Ruthie sat at a long table near the back of the second floor. She looked up when I started walking toward her, my slushy shoes squeaking on the floor. She was reading a book. As soon as she saw me, the book was closed and quickly put on the empty chair next to her. Whatever she was reading, she didn't want to share it with me.

I sat down. "Hi."

"Hi."

"How you doing?"

"Just studying. You know, for a test."

"So what'd you do with the Potassium Permangatel?"

"The what?"

"The stuff you stole from Rexall's."

"Oh. It was for a science experiment. You know, at school."

"What kind of experiment?"

She looked at me steadily for a long moment. "You going to tell Mom and Dad?"

"No."

"I appreciate that."

"You ever stolen anything before?"

"No."

"You plan on stealing anything else?"

"No."

Now I looked at her steadily for a long moment. "So what's going on, Ruthie?"

"It's just all these tests. I'm worn out. That's why I took that stuff at Rexall's. One of the girls at school told me it was really good stuff if you were run-down. Said she got all her energy back."

"So it's for energy?"

She nodded.

"I thought it was for a science experiment."

"Well, I used it for the experiment *and* for myself."

"And you didn't have enough money?"

"Right."

"Or you wouldn't have stolen it?"

"Right."

"Ruthie, we've had a charge account at Rexall for years."

"I must've forgot."

"I love you, Ruthie."

"I know you do."

"So be honest with me. Whatever it is, I want to help you."

She shrugged. "It was just for a science experiment. I must've forgotten about our charge account. I needed to get back to school right away."

I stood up. She looked happy I was going. "I'll be right back. Wait here."

I like the second floor of the library. One has the sense of timelessness there. The dust and the opaque windows, the neat and hushed rows of books. It's like being inside the time capsule they buried over at Runyon Park last summer. But the library time capsule would be filled with Chaucer and Melville and Poe and Dreiser and people like that. There was something almost religious about a life of contemplation and every once in a while I wished I was monastic. I knew it wouldn't last much longer than a day or two and then I'd be wanting to see the new Tony Curtis at the Strand or buying the new Everly Brothers record or the latest Shell Scott novel. But it was nice to think about sometimes.

I found what I wanted and came back.

"Guess what I did," I said.

"What?"

"Looked up Potassium Permangatel in the medical reference book."

"Oh."

I put my hand on hers. "Maybe we should go for a ride."

"A ride? What for?"

"So we can talk."

"We can talk here."

"No, we can't," I said.

WE WENT OUTSIDE. Four boys were having a furious snowball fight. They stopped abruptly when two girls walked by. The girls, who obviously considered themselves more mature than the boys, rolled their eyes at the very idea of snowball fights.

We walked to my car.

"Your car is always so cold," Ruthie said.

"Not in the summer."

"Very funny. And it happens to be winter."

We got in.

"God, can you turn on the heater?"

"It's on. It just takes a while to warm up,"

"I'm sorry I'm so crabby."

"You're always crabby. It's part of your charm."

"Not *this* crabby." Then, "You know, don't you?"

"Yeah. The medical reference book."

"What'd it say?"

"Well, you know, about douching."

She sighed and looked out the window. "Just what I always wanted to have. A conversation with my brother about douching."

"Maybe later we could talk about menstrual cramps."

I was driving out the river road. The ice-covered river was beautiful in the silver moonlight. The heater was roaring. It was still colder than hell in the ragtop. The seats were like ice.

"I sure hope it works," she said.

"What happened?"

"Well, then what do you *think* happened?"

"Boy, you *really* are crabby."

"I'm sorry."

"Was it, uh, all right for you?"

"You mean doing it?"

"Yeah." Doing it. My kid sister. Doing it. Sweet little Ruthie McCain.

"Does he know? The father, I mean?"

"Yes. He knows."

"You told him?"

"I wrote him a letter."

"What'd he say?"

"He said he was scared. He said this'll screw up his whole life. He wants to start in premed at the university next year."

"How about *your* life? What's supposed to happen to *your* life?"

She looked out the window some more, the way Pamela did driving home last night. You could see the paper mill along the river, big and modern and alien in the night, floodlights giving it the look of a prison. Somehow it seemed wrong, even obscene, out here on the prairie where the Indians had roamed for several hundred years.

"You going to tell me who this little bastard is?"

"First of all, he's not little. And second of all, he's not a bastard. And third of all, no, I'm not going to tell you. And it's not going to do you any good to get mad."

I couldn't believe how calm she was. "God, Ruthie, don't you want to cry or something?"

"No, do you?"

We rode along some more.

"Mind if I play the radio?" she said.

"We shouldn't listen to the radio at a time like this."

"Why not?"

"I don't know. We just shouldn't."

"Are we punishing ourselves or something?" she said.

"Maybe."

"Then can I have a cigarette?"

"A cigarette? Since when do you smoke?"

"I just smoke every once in a while. Don't worry, I don't inhale or anything."

"You're my little sister."

"And you're my big brother. What the hell does that prove?"

We rode along some more. I accidentally on purpose forgot to give her a cigarette. She didn't mention it again.

"God, I wish you hadn't found out about this."

"I'm your brother, remember?"

"We already went through that. And anyway, I'm the one who did it and it's *my* responsibility."

"Do you love him?"

She thought a moment. "I did until I saw what a little boy he is. I'm a lot more grown up than he is."

"So marriage is out?"

"Absolutely." Then, "I'll just have to try this stuff is all."

"You actually think it'll work?"

"I guess it does sometimes."

"Who said?"

"Jenny knows somebody it worked for."

"Oh, yes, Jenny, the sixteen-year-old gynecologist."

"God, I wish you hadn't found out. You're worse than he is about this."

"I just can't believe how cool you're being. Don't you *care* what happens to your future?"

"How is getting into a panic going to help me? I just have to try to think through this the best I can."

I didn't say anything for a time. Just looked out at the frozen, snow-covered river in the moonlight, sled tracks deep in the snow, the faraway small islands of birch and pine. In the summer you could see girls in bikinis all night long on those islands, headlight flashes of flesh and drunken merriment.

I looked over at my seventeen-year-old sister. She really was calm. And she was right. My intensity wasn't helping either of us. "I guess that's why you're the valedictorian of your class and I graduated with a big C-plus average."

"You're not stupid," Ruthie said.

"Face it, you got the brains in the family."

"Oh, come on."

"And the looks."

"Oh, yes, I'm a regular movie queen."

"You're beautiful and you know it."

"I'm pretty but not beautiful."

I knew at least twenty kids who'd vehemently disagree with her assessment.

I pulled onto a cliff that overlooked a cove. On the cliffs across the waters you could see some of the town's mansions.

I said, "That's where I want you to live."

"Where?"

"Over there. In one of those mansions."

"Are you crazy? I don't want to stay here."

"You don't?"

"No. What, and have three kids and a husband and get fat and cranky by the time I'm thirty. Like Aunt Tish."

Aunt Tish was legendary. On a high school trip to Hollywood right before WWII, a producer from MGM spotted her at a hamburger joint and gave her his card and asked her to make a screen test. Well, she made the test, and she was good. Not great but good, good enough anyway for MGM to offer her a short contract when she graduated high school the next year. Tish became the local celebrity. A local station even gave her a fifteen-minute radio show once a week called *Tish Tish Tish* on which she sang (not so good), told jokes that her listeners sent in (even worse) and then gave the lowdown on a lot of high school activities. The assumption being, of course, that Tish would board the train for Hollywood the day she got her diploma. But she didn't go. Her mother said that she'd gotten scared. What if she failed? What if she had to come back here in a year or so? How could she ever face all the people who had such great expectations for her? Tish started to put on weight. Nobody around here had ever seen anybody put on weight the way she did. In five months, she went from 95 pounds to 151 pounds. Mr. Berenson, the MGM man, kept calling long-distance and asking her what the holdup was. They were doing a Betty Grable musical set on a college campus and Tish would be perfect for a small part as one of the freshman girls. Then Tish broke down and told him about her weight problem. Mr. Berenson was most sympathetic, but after her confession, he didn't linger on the phone. Nor did she ever hear from him again. She stayed in town. Within one year, she weighed 170 pounds which, at five-one, was considerable. She got married to a milkman, had three kids bing-bing-bing and then got a local religious radio show in which she, among other things, reviewed movies through "God's perspective." At least she'd given up singing and telling jokes. She was still around: Aunt Tish, a dour woman who always brought terrible potato salad to family reunions and always managed to bring up her near-miss in Hollywood.

"I want to be a lawyer, like you."

"Oh, yes. A big success like me.' "

"I want to go to law school at the U of I because the tuition's so cheap, and then I want to go to Chicago and join a really prestigious firm."

"What about kids?"

"I want kids. But not now. And not 'til I get my career going."

"You sound like Ayn Rand."

"It's nineteen fifty-nine. Girls can do a lot more than they used to."

I heard the motorcycle before I saw it. At first, I didn't think enough about it to look down the dark, winding road for it. There are a lot of motorcycles in a town like ours. Personally, I prefer custom cars. They're my weakness. But motorcycles are fine, too, except for the ones with all the saddlebags and air horns and plastic streamers on the handle grips.

The flashing red light caused me to turn my head. The flashing red light, mounted on the fender of the big Indian, also announced who it was, one Chief Cliff Sykes, Jr.

Cliff goes to a lot of cowboy movies and it shows. While the rest of his sixteen-man force wear the traditional blue of the police officer, Cliffie prefers the kind of tight khaki uniform Glen Ford likes to wear in westerns, sort of a modern-day gunfighter's outfit. He wears his Colt that way, too, in a holster slung low over his right hip. And he has a mustache, a black line that per-

fectly traces the arc of his insolent mouth. He wears cowboy
boots made out of rattlesnake skin. And he carries a Bowie knife
in a scabbard that hangs off the back of his belt. He's shot and
killed five men in the six years he's been chief. A lot of people,
including me, think the killings didn't need to happen, that a little
police know-how and patience would have brought the incidents
to a more humane conclusion. He's also famous for getting con-
fessions out of innocent people. Cliff, Sr., his father, controls a lot
of jobs in this town and when you put a grand jury together,
you're always looking at a number of people whose fates are one
way or the other in the hands of Cliff's father. So are they going
to charge Cliffie with excessive force? Not likely.

He got off his motorcycle, emergency light flashing. For all his
affectations and little-boy tough-guy stuff, all the silly B-movie
stuff, he truly was a spooky guy because he took a pornographic
pleasure in the pain and suffering of others. There's smart evil
and there's dumb evil in this world of ours. Smart evil conspires
and plots and manipulates; dumb evil just reaches out and grabs.
Cliffie was definitely dumb evil.

He shone his light in the window. The beam revealed Ruthie
first and then me. The huge flashlight was actually a club and he
often used it that way. He knocked on the window.

I rolled it down. "Something I can do for you?"

"Yeah," he said, "but I can't say it in front of your little sister."
A car went by, headlights angling through the darkness, slowing
down when it reached us, trying to figure out what little Cliffie
was doing. Anywhere that Cliffie went, excitement was sure to
follow.

"In fact, McCain, get out of the car."

"Why?"

"Why?" he said, slapping his flashlight in the palm of his hand.
"A, because I said to, and B, because I said to. That clear enough
for you?"

I looked over at Ruthie. "I'll be fine." I wanted to reassure her,
just in case she was scared.

"Gee, all he said was he wanted you to step out of the car. He didn't say he was going to shoot you or anything."

"Sensible girl, your little sister," Sykes said, smirking.

I got out of the car.

"Let's take a walk."

"To where?" I said.

"Just along the road." Then, "Oh, you got a weed?"

That was another thing about Cliffie. He never bought what he could mooch. He probably hadn't bought a pack of cigarettes since he'd graduated from high school. "Light?" he said, after I handed him the smokes. I gave him my Ronson. He lit up and handed the lighter back.

We might have been two friends out strolling for an evening, just walking along, looking out at the moon-silver river, the big pavilion just ahead of us. You could hear the summer echoes, kids and their folks laughing and dogs barking and radios blasting and cars honking merrily as they pulled in loaded with more families and more dogs and more hot dogs and more Pepsi.

He got me in the ribs with his flashlight and doubled me over. It was the second shot, the one in the stomach, that dropped me to my knees.

"Counselor's been a bad boy," he said. And then kicked me quickly in the groin.

I'm not much of a pain fan. I know that some people think that spiritual growth can come from pain but I'll leave that for the philosophers to figure out. I just don't like pain—not from a dentist, not from a surgeon, not from a drunk, and not from a psychotic chief of police who once told a local fawning radio reporter that he considered his job that of "town tamer, you know, like Wyatt Earp and Bill Tilden and all those men."

"You were supposed to wait at the murder scene 'til I told you you could go."

I didn't say anything. He circled me. When he got square with my back, he gave me a wedge of rattlesnake boot in the kidney. I cried out.

"That's the first thing that pissed me off today, McCain. The second thing was you starting the story that Kenny Whitney didn't kill his wife."

At which point, I got another boot toe driven deep into my kidney.

Ruthie suddenly lurched from the car and said, "You leave my brother alone, you asshole. And I don't care if you're the chief of police or not." I guess she really had believed he was just going to talk to me.

"Nice talk for a young lady," Sykes said.

"Get back in the car, Ruthie. Please."

"He doesn't have any right to hit you."

"We'll talk about it later, Ruthie. Please just get back in the car now."

"You asshole," she said to Sykes.

"I could run you in," Sykes said. "Talking to a lawman like that."

"Too bad I don't have a necktie, then you could tie me to the jail cell and beat me." A few years back, Sykes, Sr., had arrested Lem Tompkins, a hardware store clerk who was a rival for Sykes, Jr.'s girlfriend. Sykes, Sr., accused Tompkins of driving while intoxicated then took him back to the cell where he tied him to the bars and beat him pretty badly. Lem ended up in the hospital for a week. Sykes, Sr., somehow managed to convince the town that Lem, who'd been in trouble for breaking and entering a few years back, had attacked Sykes, Sr. Judge Whitney demanded Sykes' resignation. But the town was in a bind—their choice being the cold, imperious arrogance of the old money Whitneys versus the cold, imperious arrogance of the new-money barbarians at the gate as represented by the Sykes family. It isn't much of a choice but I guess I'd lean toward the upper-crust intelligence of the Whitneys. The town leaned toward the Sykeses. Sykes, Sr., kept his job.

Ruthie finally got back in the car. I just kept thinking of her pregnant. Little Ruthie. My kid sister. Knocked up.

"Now, this is a nice simple case of murder and suicide," Sykes was saying. "And anybody who says anything different is full of shit. Including that bitch you work for. She's just trying to salvage what she can of her family's reputation. Well, Counselor, I could give a shit about her family's reputation. There's going to be an inquest in the morning and I want this whole thing wrapped up by noon and I don't want any interference from you or your boss. She was shot four times with the thirty-two we found four feet from her body. The county doc tells me that death was probably instantaneous. Then you got there and talked to Whitney and he went upstairs and shot himself. We understand each other, Counselor?"

I was cold, I had to pee, my ribs felt broken and my kidney felt on fire. My nose was running from the wind. I felt humiliated, and angry. Someday, I was going to have the pleasure of smacking Cliffie in the face, and to hell with the consequences.

"We understand each other, Counselor? I hear any more stories about Kenny not being the one who killed Susan, I'm running you in. Got that?"

He stood in front of me now, over me. He looked like he was enjoying my cigarette pretty well. "Now, get on your feet so I can walk you back to your car."

Pain had silenced me. Getting to me feet was difficult. At one point, I thought I might pitch over backward, but I kept pushing my legs to stand straight up. Finally, I was able to stand up without wobbling.

We walked back to my car, our footsteps loud as they crunched gravel. We moved much more slowly than before.

"She's not going to do it to me again, Counselor. And neither are you. This is one murder case that I've got in the bag."

Cliffie and Judge Whitney have this game: he arrests somebody for murder and she hires me to prove that the person is innocent. She doesn't care about justice any more than Cliffie does. He just wants an arrest so he can close the case and prove to the town that he's a detection wizard; she just wants to humiliate him. If somebody innocent gets hurt in the cross fire, so be it. Neither cares. Their war has been going on for a long time now and is likely to continue.

At the car, he said, "Tell Judge Whitney she doesn't have to be at the inquest tomorrow. Everything is laid out. I'll be there and so will the county attorney." He smiled. "My cousin Phil." Then, "Oh, and Judge Hardy. He'll be there, too. I kept trying to get to Judge Whitney but seems she was in meetings all day."

An inquest like this would generally fall under Judge Whitney's jurisdiction, but Cliffie was way ahead of us. He'd gotten his crony Judge Hardy and his cousin the county attorney to preside over the inquest. Being beneficiaries of the Sykeses' largesse, they'd say whatever Cliffie told them to.

I got in the car. He held the door open. He kept looking at Ruthie. He probably imagined that she found him sexy. His gun hand rode on the bone handle of his holstered weapon. "You're the smart one in the family, Ruthie. You tell this brother of yours to stay out of trouble. All right?"

She just glared at him.

Cliffie grinned. "Well, good night. And be sure to give my best to your folks."

"Are you all right?" Ruthie said as soon as I closed the door.

"I'll live."

"But that's illegal, what he did."

"I'm all right, Ruthie." I reached over and patted her hand. "Really."

"That's the kind of person I'm going after when I'm a lawyer. The man who hides behind the law. They're the worst kind of law."

"Right now, I'm more worried about your situation than I am about Cliffie."

I started my car. It trembled to life. I gave it a quarter-inch of choke. After a few seconds in which nothing seemed to happen, in which the motor continued to tremble, the choke kicked in and the gas flow evened out and the motor ran smoothly.

Sykes was gone by now. I drove back to town. The windows in the houses gleamed silver with flickering TV images. Every once in a while you'd see teenagers walking with skates slung over their shoulders, headed for the rink. I had KOMA on the radio.

They were playing nothing but Buddy Holly and Richie Valens and rock stars were calling in and saying how great those guys had been and how much they'd be missed.

I looked over at Ruthie. "So what're you going to do?"

"Try the potassium."

"When?"

"Probably tomorrow."

"You let me know right away."

"Just don't tell anybody."

"God, are you crazy? Who would I tell?"

"Does that mean you're ashamed of me?"

She wasn't as cool inside as she was trying to pretend. "Of course I'm not ashamed of you. You're my sister. I love you."

"You don't think I'm a whore?"

"Of course not."

"Well, sometimes I wonder if maybe I'm not."

"You slept with one boy. That's hardly being a whore."

"One-and-a-half."

"Huh?"

"Remember Roger?"

"The kid with the stutter?"

"Yeah."

"I let him get to somewhere between second and third base."

"Oh."

"But only once. At a New Year's Eve party when we were sophomores. And I'd had some wine."

"That still doesn't make you a whore."

"Sometimes I just worry that Father Gillis is right."

"You mean about how most girls who go all the way in high school end up in Chicago as prostitutes?" I said.

" 'Prosties."

"Huh?"

"That's what Father Gillis calls them."

"Oh."

"So he sounds like he knows what he's talking about. You

know, like Frank Sinatra or somebody. He gave the girls this lecture about a year ago. After mass one Sunday."

"If every girl in this town who went all the way in high school ended up in Chicago on the streets, there wouldn't be room for anybody else to walk."

She giggled. Then, "I'm not a whore."

"I know you're not."

"But that's what people'd say if they found out."

I pulled up in the driveway of our folks' place. I leaned over and kissed her on the cheek. "This'll all work out."

"Maybe the potassium'll really work."

She kissed me back on the cheek then slid out of the car. "I'll call you tomorrow. And thanks for being such a nice brother."

"My pleasure."

"And Cliffie is still an asshole."

On the way over to my place, I played the radio real loud. I tried to drive all thought of Ruthie from my mind. The potassium wasn't going to work. I didn't know if anything would work. This was going to devastate my whole family.

TWELVE

Mrs. Goldman's house had once been what she laughingly called "a starter mansion," meaning that it was a lot more house than she and her husband could afford at the time, but not enough of a house to qualify as one of the true mansions you saw on the other side of town. Mr. Goldman, who was in the real estate business, didn't live long enough to make his final fortune. He left his wife, Sandra, enough term insurance to pay off the house and support herself by taking in boarders. The place was a two-story gingerbread Victorian. I had half of the huge upstairs as my apartment. I also had a stall in the garage and my own back entrance for when I came in late. Two meals, breakfast and dinner, were included in the price of the rent. Mrs. Goldman was a great cook. She was also a frustrated writer and photographer. She was always working on her history of the town. She was doing a great job. We'd spent a lot of long nights together watching her TV set and talking about her book and the plans I have for when my law practice gets rolling.

When I came into the vestibule tonight, I peeked through the French doors on the first floor. She was sitting in a chair reading a novel. The TV was on but the sound was turned down. She'd explained once that it was like having company you didn't have to pay any attention to. She was a tall, slender, striking woman in her early fifties. She'd been dating a dentist from Cedar Rapids for several years but I didn't have the sense that marriage was imminent.

She waved me in.

"You missed a nice meal."

"Sorry."

"Meat loaf." Then she smiled. "There's enough left for a sandwich later if you get hungry. I'll make it for you if you want."

"Well, I'm going to that skating party."

"Oh, those poor singers. The rock and roll ones."

"Yes."

She shook her elegant head. She wore a white blouse, a dramatic black belt, gray slacks and black flats. When Lauren Bacall gets older, she'll probably look something like Mrs. Goldman. If she's lucky. "And poor Susan Whitney."

"I didn't know you knew her."

"Oh, you know, from Leopold Bloom's. As you know, I don't care for the couple that run it, but it is a pleasant place to spend an hour or two occasionally. Especially if they're not there and it's just a clerk."

I thought of Steve Renauld and his relationship with Susan Whitney and of her remark that she could only sleep with men she felt sorry for.

"The kind of man her husband was, I guess I'm not surprised," she said.

Maybe at breakfast I'd tell her my theory that Kenny hadn't killed her. For now, I wanted to get my skates and head for the rink. I was hoping to see Pamela there.

"Well, I'll talk to you in the morning."

"How come you're limping?"

Maybe I'd tell her about Cliffie, too, in the morning. "Oh, I slipped on the ice."

She put her novel on her lap and leaned forward in the chair. "Say, did you come home about three-thirty this afternoon?"

"No, why?"

"I thought I heard somebody up in your room. I can't be sure. But I thought I heard footsteps up there and then something scraping the floor."

"It wasn't Andrea?" Andrea being the English teacher who rents the other half of the upstairs. She teaches at the state-run school for the deaf. She's one of those secretive women who always look vaguely frightened. She lugs home armloads of mystery novels from the library, Mignon Eberhardt seeming to be her favorite, and rarely says a word.

"No, she doesn't get home until at least four-thirty."

I raised my eyes to the ceiling, as if I had X-ray vision and could see through the floor right into my apartment. It'd be pretty cool to be Superman. Just beam your eyes right through the floor. But among my many goals, turning myself into Superman was probably the least achievable. "This was about three-thirty?"

"Yes. And it wasn't you?"

"No, no it wasn't me."

"I could've been mistaken."

"I'll go have a look."

"I hope I don't seem like some old busybody."

I smiled. "Hardly."

"Would you like me to come up there with you?"

"No, I'll be fine."

"I have my husband's handgun from the war."

"I appreciate it. But that's fine."

"I'll be happy to give you the gun. It's a forty-five."

It came into my head, then, something that had been wedged in there uncomfortably ever since Cliffie had put it there about forty-five minutes ago. He said that Susan had been killed with a .32. But the gun Kenny had fired at me through the window, and the gun he used to kill himself with, was a .45. So where had the .32 come from? And I hadn't seen a .32 anywhere in the house.

"Are you all right?"

"Fine," I said. "I just thought of something." Then, "Well, I guess I'll go upstairs."

"You sure you don't want the gun?"

"Even if there was somebody up there, he's long gone by now."

We talked a bit more and then I closed the French doors and started up the stairs that rose from the vestibule. I clicked on the stairway light, something I don't always do, and went up the steps. I could tell Andrea was home because there was a line of light beneath her door. Otherwise I'd have had no idea if she was home or not. She was utterly silent. The other door, down the hall from hers, was mine. The line beneath it was dark. I put my ear to the door and listened. Nothing. Absolutely nothing.

I used my key and let myself in. Darkness. I had two large rooms and a bath. The only light came through a window from a streetlight a quarter block away. I walked toward it. There was a table with a lamp to the side of that window. I clicked on the light.

If there had been somebody in here, he or she was awfully neat. At least in the living room. Nothing whatsoever looked different or disordered. Mrs. Goldman keeps my place very neat. She raised two sons and always says the trick with boys is never let their rooms go more than two days unchecked. So she dusts and vacuums and picks up twice a week before the governor has to declare my place an official disaster area.

It's a pleasant furnished apartment. The furniture isn't new but it's clean and comfortable and the place was wallpapered fresh only a month before I moved in. When the window's open, you can still smell the fresh wallpaper paste, which is a smell I'm inexplicably fond of. There's a great shower and a very firm mattress. My favorite spot is the recliner where I read my crime paperbacks. There's a lamp that hangs right over my shoulder for plenty of light, and a small table to my left where I can set my ashtray and Pall Malls and a can of beer or a Pepsi. Now if I just had Pamela living here with me. . .

I tried the bedroom. Nothing looked disturbed in there, either. The cats trailed behind me. They didn't want to miss anything. I half-expected one of them to put on her deerstalker cap and the other to produce a magnifying glass. They'd probably have better luck than I was having.

Where it went wrong was in the bedroom closet. Just last night I'd set a pair of loafers down on the floor to take to the shoe repair shop for new heels. I remembered doing this. There was no mistake. But the shoes had been sat back up on the closet shelf with two pairs of old tennis shoes. The intruder had gotten confused and figured that all three pairs of shoes belonged on the shelf. Somebody had been in here.

I was just about to switch off the bedroom light and go back to the living room when I noticed the shoe print on the floor. It looked familiar but at first I wasn't sure why. The dirty snow he'd tracked in had made the shoe impression clear.

I went over to my bedside table; I keep a flashlight there. It isn't half the size of Cliffie's but it's handy and serviceable when there's a power outage or I hear strange noises in the darkness. The noises usually turn out to be raccoons. I made the mistake of putting out food for a couple of baby raccoons one night, and now I have a whole family of them working their way up my back stairs several nights a week. But they're all so cute I can't break it off.

I followed the footprints from my bedroom to the door. The pattern of the prints resembled a waffle iron. An image came to me: Robert Frazier, sitting in the leather chair across from Judge Whitney, and the imposing, expensive winter shoes he wore. I remembered thinking they looked like rubber cleats. They'd make a pattern similar to the one on my floor. But why the hell would Frazier be in my apartment? What would he be looking for?

I felt better. Yes, there'd been an intruder in my apartment and yes, I now knew who it had been. Or thought I did, anyway. Now, all I needed to know was why he'd been up here.

I went and got my skates. They were black and dusty. At least the blades looked reasonably sharp. A skater, I'm not. I changed clothes, too, jeans and a button-down blue shirt and a black pullover sweater. I was glad to get out of my suit and tie. They always feel confining to me and I feel like an impostor in them, like I'm a kid pretending to be a grown-up. Which, come to think of it, maybe I am.

As I changed clothes, the two cats sat on the bureau watching me. I wasn't all that interesting but the TV wasn't on so I'd have to do. They have their programs. For some unfathomable feline reason, they loved westerns, especially the gunplay and the cattle stampedes.

I tossed my skates over my shoulder as casually as I could, hoping I resembled one of those ski bums you always see in whiskey ads. You know, the ones with the perfect teeth. For what they've spent on their teeth, we could build several new schools.

A few minutes later, I was down in the driveway trying to get the car to run smoothly. I kept using the choke and swearing a lot. That was a combination that always seemed to work.

THIRTEEN

THE SKATING RINK WAS packed. I had to park on a graveled shelf looking down on the rink. Parking spots were hard to find.

It's a great rink, built just a few years ago. The rink itself is kidney-shaped, carved out of a plot of timber that runs to firs and jack pines and hardwoods. On the southeast edge of the rink is the warming house, a log cabin–style structure where you can buy hot chocolate, hot dogs, popcorn and Pepsi, plus get warm around an old-fashioned potbellied stove. Probably the prettiest the rink ever looks is at holiday time. Two nights before Christmas, there's a costume pageant of people on skates. It's probably not quite up to Broadway standards but it's pretty to watch and the choir always sounds great. The rink is a place where a lot of romances start and a lot of romances end. The couple you saw last year positively enraptured with each other are this year enduring sporadic fights and glowering silences. Or they're with new mates.

The music over the loudspeakers was a lot better than usual tonight. Out here, they play a lot of music that was popular five years ago, like the Ames Brothers and Eddie Fisher. They can't quite bring themselves to play rock and roll unless it's by the

Chipmunks or the McGuire Sisters, but tonight, the air was filled with Buddy Holly and "That'll Be the Day" and, man, it made me feel great, all charged up and convinced that Pamela Forrest was going to fall in love with me.

She would, anyway, if I could ever find her.

I spent my first half-hour skating around the rink looking for her. To no avail. Not a sign of her on the rink or in the warming house.

As for the skating, I stuck to the outside of the rink. Fewer people noticed me falling down that way. Every once in a while, I'd get going pretty well and I'd think that I'd suddenly somehow mastered the ice, and then the ice would dump me again. It's not good for your ego to have five-year-old girls giggle and point at you. I was going to give them the bird but then I thought that that probably wouldn't look real mature on my part.

I was thinking about going home—I was spending more time on my butt than on my blades—when Mary Travers slipped an arm through mine and drew me out into the center of the rink where the grown-ups and young show-offs were skating. She smelled wonderful, and looked even better, her jaunty raspberry-colored beret angled beautifully across her silky chestnut-colored hair and her cheeks tinted with the night's air. She wore a heavy turtleneck sweater that matched her beret, jeans and a pair of white high-top skates that flashed artfully whenever she made one of her elegant, practiced moves.

"You should hire me, McCain."

"For what?"

"To teach you how to skate."

"You don't think I'm any good?"

"I saw those little girls laughing at you."

"Yes, and I'm planning to sue them, too."

She laughed and squeezed my arm tighter and took me around the rink. It was fun. I didn't have to do anything. She was strong and fleet enough for both of us.

She said, "I don't see Pamela anywhere."

"Well, I don't see our friendly druggist—i.e., your fiancé—any-where, either."

"He's at a city council meeting."

I was going to say something snide but decided against it. She deserved her happiness. She was the most decent person I'd ever known, and if I could have, I would have fallen in love with her in a second. I wanted her to be happy.

"Does he know you're here?" I said.

"No."

"How'd you manage that?"

"I didn't. I just told him I wasn't sure what I was going to do."

"So you came out here?"

"Looks that way, doesn't it?" She smiled but I could see the sadness in her eyes this time, the sadness I always put there with-out meaning to.

We skated some more. I kept looking around for Pamela.

Mary said, "I really don't want to marry him, McCain."

"I know."

"He always reminds me I'm from the Knolls, like he's doing me a favor or something by marrying me."

"So why don't you just call it off?"

"I want kids."

"His kids?"

"Well. . ."

We skated some more. She kept good strong hold of my arm. You could smell stove smoke from the warming house and every once in a while somebody would skate by with a hot dog and you could smell mustard and ketchup.

"He's going to build them a house."

"Build who a house?" I said.

"My folks."

"He's going to build your folks a house?"

"That's going to be my wedding present."

"Wow."

"He owns this land up on Ridgedale, where they're putting in a new development. That's where he's going to build it. They'll be out of the Knolls and into a brand-new house. He's even going to furnish it for them."

I looked at her. "And he's going to hold it over your head the rest of your life."

A male voice came on the loudspeaker and said, "We'd like to have a moment's silence to commemorate the deaths of the fine young men who died in a plane crash not very far from here."

And I kind of felt it, even though all the other stuff was going on, Kenny and Susan dead and Ruthie pregnant and Mary marrying the wrong man—even with all that turmoil, there was still room to think about Buddy Holly and Richie Valens and the Bopper and to feel sorry for them and their families. I know they say that young men consider themselves invincible. I guess that changed for me a couple of years ago when I was doing my stint as a weekend warrior with the National Guard. I'd wanted to go on to law school so the Guard was the only way I could avoid the draft.

One rainy Saturday when I was off-loading a supply truck in the warehouse, this skinny kid from Cedar Rapids hops in another truck and tromps on the gas. He always liked to lay down a strip of rubber in reverse. The sound echoing off the warehouse ceiling was pretty cool, I had to admit. He always ended his routine by coming within inches of the wall behind him and then slamming on the brakes. Everybody liked to watch him. He was a crazy son of a bitch. But this one day Belaski, this Polish farmer, he was walking behind the truck when the kid was backing up at sixty miles an hour. And the kid didn't see Belaski and, no matter how loud we screamed, he didn't hear us *warning* him about Belaski, either. It's a terrible way to put it, but he just squashed Belaski against the concrete block wall like a bug. Belaski popped and oozed like a bug, too. The major on duty that weekend made me and my friend and fellow law-school partner Dick Freidman clean up with a hose after the ambulance took Belaski away. No more sense of invincibility for me. Not ever again. And I thought of Belaski now as Mary and I stood there on the skating rink. And I got sad and scared and confused the way I do sometimes because no matter how we try to explain it—through religion or randomness, it doesn't matter—existence just doesn't seem to make any sense. I had a philosophy instructor at the U of I say that the only question that mattered in all of philosophy was Verlaine's "Why are we born to suffer and die?" All else was irrelevant, my instructor said. And sometimes, without wanting to, I let myself slip into that frame of mind. But I never stayed there long. I was afraid to. Even if it all ultimately means nothing, you've got to play the game not only for yourself but for the people you love.

Like looking around at the rink now. All the generations. And mostly good people, too. Handing down the best and most sacred things from one era to another. They made me feel good, these people, watching them tonight. They had a real dignity, the grandfather showing the five-year-old how to skate, the ten-year-old boy blushing when the girl next door took his hand, the six or seven black couples up here with their kids, joining in and being welcomed. Maybe life didn't make sense but then it was our business, I guess, to *impose* meaning on it.

I said, "How about a walk?"

"Sure. Where?"

"Oh. Through the woods, I guess. There's a full moon and plenty of light."

"Great," she said.

So we changed into our boots and went for a walk.

We found a winding trail through the low-hanging boughs, still heavy with snow that gleamed blue and silver in the moonlight. The noise and lights of the rink stayed with us for a time, like a memory you don't quite want to let go of, but then we were in the darker woods, and the silence was deep and wide, broken only by the crunch of our footsteps on the snow and sticks in the path. I knew this area pretty well. My dad and I used to hunt out here. He wasn't very good and I was worse and in all our years of trying, I don't think we ever got anything, which was fine with me. I look at dead deer roped across car roofs and it either pisses me off or depresses me.

We came to an open field at the base of a steep, clay cliff. There was a small circular pond where kids swim in the summer. They also push rowboats and canoes in the water and play around. The pond is too small for motor boats. It was pretty, the pond, and the snow ridged around it, all shimmery and gleaming in the moonlight. The cliffs looked rugged and red and the jack pines atop them were silhouetted perfectly against the winter clouds. Far off, you could hear dogs, and then semis on the highways and then, closer by, the faded forlorn bay of a coyote.

"God, it's great out here," Mary said. And then scooped up some snow and made a snowball. "Bet you I can hit that canoe."

"Bet you can't."

The canoe was a remnant of summer, like the pair of cheap cracked sunglasses you find in the glove compartment around Christmastime, or the tube of suntan lotion you find wrenched like a tube of toothpaste in the back of the medicine cabinet. Somebody had left the canoe here and it sat in the middle of the pond looking silly and somehow pathetic in its uselessness.

But it made a great snowball target.

"Here goes," she said.

She didn't come close, but she came close enough to surprise me.

"Now you try, McCain."

"I hate to show off."

"In other words, you can't do it either."

God, she looked so great just then, she was the pretty girl up in the Knolls again, young and vital and sweet.

I made a snowball. "Stand back. The velocity'll probably knock you on your butt."

"Uh-huh."

"And there'll be pieces of debris flying all over when I hit the canoe."

"Uh-huh."

"Yeah, well, we'll see whose saying 'uh-huh' after I hit it."

"Uh-huh."

I was Bob Feller of the Cleveland Indians. I could throw a ball

faster than any man alive. And more accurately, too. I was Bob
Feller and I was really going to show her my stuff.

I cocked my arm back and threw.

The snowball arced high and looked as if it was going to skid
away south of the canoe. But then it dipped abruptly and came
down, landing very near the aft end of the target.

"Nice, McCain, but not good enough. How about giving me
one more throw?"

"You already had your throw."

"Afraid I'll beat you?"

"Hardly."

"Then give me one more chance."

She was too pretty to say no to. "All right. One more."

She made another snowball, packing it good and tight in her
red mittens. "I'm going to humiliate you."

"Sure."

"I am." Then, "Here goes, McCain."

The throw was good but not great. Or that's what I smugly
told myself a few seconds after the snowball left her mitten. But
when I saw the trajectory I got this funny feeling that maybe it
was great after all. We watched it go up and we watched it come
down. Mine had just fallen suddenly from the sky. Hers fell in a
graceful downward curve. Even before it landed, she was jump-
ing up and down and slugging me in the arm the way girls do.

From here, it was impossible to tell whose snowball had come
closer to the canoe. We were talking less than an inch of difference probably, both snowballs having gone *splat* very close to the
canoe itself.

"I won!" she said.

"Too close to call. We'll have to go look."

"Is it safe? The ice, I mean?"

"Probably."

"Boy, that's really reassuring, McCain."

"I'll go check."

"Oh, McCain—"

She grabbed me and held on to me. "You sure you want to do this over some stupid snowball contest?"

Every other winter around here, somebody drowns trying to walk out on the ice. One year, two teenaged valedictorians drove their car out on the ice. I didn't want to be this year's dummy. "I'll just go out a foot or so. See what it's like."

"Just be very careful."

"I will."

We walked over to the snowbound rise above the pond and then stepped ponderously down the small hill until we reached the ice.

"You really want to do this?"

"I'll be fine."

But talking about it sort of spooked me. What if I walked out there and dropped straight down to my icy death?

I decided to get it over with. I walked to the pond's edge, and for some reason looked up at the full moon. And just then the coyote chose to cry again. And that spooked me a little. Maybe he knew something I didn't. Maybe he had psychic powers, the way those ads in the magazines claim you can have for only $1.99. Or you can get a truss or a bust enhancer, just in case you're a little skeptical of the psychic powers deal.

I went out one foot, two feet, three feet. It felt as solid as the rink ice.

"C'mon back, McCain. Don't go any further."

"It's perfectly safe."

"I thought I heard a crack," she half-shouted.

"It's your imagination."

"C'mon, McCain, please come back."

"I'll be fine."

And I was.

I got bolder with each step. The ice felt perfectly solid. I kept walking toward the canoe. I even put on a little skit for Mary. "Oh, my God! The ice is cracking!" And I started windmilling my arms like I was going to sink into the water.

"McCain! McCain!"

"I'm just kidding. I'm fine."

And to demonstrate that I was fine, I slid across the ice on my boots, right up to the canoe. Oh, I was the dashing one, I was, showing off for a girl the way I used to try and show off back in seventh grade. I was pretty good at sliding, too. I put on a regular show for her; all the while she kept shouting at me to be careful. And all the while I enjoyed her shouting because it made me feel so manly, the carefree adventurer striking terror in the heart of the woman who loves him so much. Move over, Robert Mitchum.

And that's when both things happened. I saw the dead girl in the canoe. And the blood all over her tan skirt. And I felt the ice start to fold under me. And that crack that Mary had mentioned hearing? Well, all of a sudden, I was hearing it, too.

And then Mary wasn't alone. Shouting, I mean. I was shouting, too.

Could I pull myself back up without pulling the entire canoe down on top of me and sinking myself to the bottom of the deep, dark pond?

PART II

FOURTEEN

Don't panic: those were the two words I remembered from Boy Scout camp. When you find yourself in a dangerous situation, keep your head and don't panic.

But of course I panicked. Natural human reaction after being dumped into deep and icy water.

I wrapped my arms around the end of the canoe and hung on. I did my best not to move. Every time I shifted even slightly, I heard the ice crack some more.

I could hear Mary hollering for help and that was about all.

And then I took hold. The rational part of me did, anyway. I decided that if I could stay absolutely still I'd be all right. I occupied my time by trying to get a better look at the dead girl in the canoe. I thought of the girl missing the next county over. There was at least a chance it was her.

Mary was at the canoe, jerking a wooden oar out. Walking carefully over to me. I guess her slight weight kept her from breaking through the ice.

She pushed the oar at me and said, "Just grab on to it, McCain."

"Thanks, Mary."

It always looks easy in the movies but it's not, pulling yourself out of icy water with whatever safety device is thrown to you. For one thing, you're cold and soaked and about as mobile as a block of concrete. For another, your hands are numb, so it's hard to get a grip on anything.

Mary stayed calm. And she looked very pretty doing it, her cocked beret and elegant face outlined in the moonlight. But she was all work: no slacking, no wasted words. She was slowly pulling me back to the ice again.

I finally got the middle of my body even with the ice and, between her pulling on the oar and me grappling with my elbows, I was able to pull myself up. I collapsed on the ice for a few moments, my breath coming in terrible shaken gasps. I heard the noises my lungs and throat were making. I didn't know human beings could make noises like that.

"I don't know how strong this part of the ice is," she said. "Maybe you'd better get up now, McCain."

"God, thanks for saving me."

"I couldn't just let you drown," she said. She smiled. "Though sometimes I've thought about it."

I slowly got to my feet. "What's that sound?"

"Your teeth."

"My teeth?"

"They're chattering."

I hadn't known until that very moment that teeth actually do chatter.

The flashlights were like insect eyes coming at us through the dark woods. All I could think of were those hokey earth-invasion movies at the drive-in. I just hoped these folks wouldn't be wearing papier-mâché masks. They'd heard Mary's calls.

They came out of the woods in silhouette. You could see their silver breath and you could see the insistent bobbing eyes of their flashlights. But there was no human detail. They could have been phantoms.

They were shouting now, mostly things like "Are you all right?"

A few of them hit the ice and started walking tentatively

toward us. One of the women had thought to bring a blanket. When she saw me standing there soaked from the waist down, she forgot about the ice and walked out to me. She threw the blanket over my shoulders. "Bring that thermos over here!" she called to somebody on the edge of the pond.

Matt Tjaden was the man who brought the thermos out. He's the county attorney and plans to run for governor someday, sooner rather than later. He was the Kiwanis Club's Man of the Year for the entire midwest two years ago. The only club I've joined since reaching my majority is the Science Fiction Book Club, which is to say that Tjaden and I don't have a lot in common. I suspect he's a decent guy when he's not being official, but I've never had the chance to find out. He's the stalking horse for the Sykes clan and I'm the unofficial representative of the Whitneys.

"I've always said you were all wet," Tjaden said. "And now you've proven my point."

"Har de har har," another guy said. "Just give him the damn coffee, Matt, and spare him the jokes."

Tjaden has the kind of bland Van Johnson good looks that old ladies like and men don't dislike. He probably believes at least half the corny things he espouses, and if he isn't especially bright, he also isn't especially mean or vindictive, which is a lot more than you can say for the Sykes clan. The only time he can get you down is on the Fourth of July when he gives his inevitable death penalty speech right before the fireworks. If Tjaden had his way, we'd be hanging people every other week. Tjaden sees our state's unwillingness to execute more people as "the subtle and nefarious influence of Communism." The quote by the way is from J. Edgar Hoover. I think Tjaden carries a photo of J. Edgar in his wallet.

Tonight, Tjaden looked like a skiing ad in *Esquire* magazine. He had on some very fancy red and blue ski togs and some blue boots that came up to his knees. He looked like a superhero in a comic book. Except for his slight jowls. And slight paunch. And slight baldness. And slight nearsightedness. After he poured me a

cup of coffee, he started telling people to go back to the rink, that
everything was under control here.

I said, "There's something we need to talk about."

"You should be more careful, McCain."

"Thanks for the tip."

"You'd never catch me out on this ice."

"I hate to point this out," I said, shivering inside my blanket,
"but you're on this ice now."

"Oh," he said, and then looked down at the ice. "Well, you
know, I meant standing where the ice is weak."

"There's a body in the canoe over there."

"What?"

"A body."

"Dead?"

"No, she's sunbathing."

"Who is she?"

"I was going to find out but then the ice gave way."

He looked over at the canoe. "You think it's safe to go over
there?"

"If we walk wide and come in from the north."

"God, this town is going to hell in a handbasket. First, Kenny
Whitney goes nuts and kills his wife and himself, and now there's
a dead girl in a canoe."

What I really wanted to do was go home and soak in a hot
bath and drink some brandy while steaming out the head cold
that was already mounting a cavalry charge.

Tjaden wouldn't go to the canoe. I had to do it. This time, I got
a good look at the girl. She wasn't at all familiar. She was probably Ruthie's age. She had on a winter coat but it was open. I had
an irrational thought, about how cold she must be. I wanted to
put my blanket on her. Then I remembered that she was dead.

I moved closer. In the moonlight, the blood that soaked her tan
skirt looked black. There was blood all over her hands and legs.
Her white blouse was clean, as was her face. I wondered what
could have caused this much blood.

I walked back up and grabbed the stern of the canoe and dragged it across the ice. I pulled it up on the snowy shore.

"God Almighty," Tjaden said. "Look at that blood."

I didn't say anything.

"What the hell happened?"

"I don't know."

"You see any bullet holes or cuts or anything?"

"Nope."

"Me either," he said.

Then he got pious on me. "The way girls run around today, just like our pastor says, you dress like a whore, people are just naturally going to think you are a whore."

"She isn't dressed like a whore."

"If she'd stayed home and done her schoolwork at night, she wouldn't be in this canoe right now."

"What if she died during the day?"

He shook his head. "She didn't die during the day."

"How do you know?"

"I can just tell is all."

Who needs scientific detection when you've got Tjaden around?

I heard voices.

To my right, coming down the hill from the gravel road that fronted this section of timber, I could see more flashlights bobbing in the gloom.

"Looks like Cliff," Tjaden said.

"Thank God," I said. "We're all saved."

"He's a lot better lawman than you give him credit for, McCain."

"That wouldn't be hard, since I don't give him any credit at all."

It was Cliffie all right, gunbelt slung low, cigarette dangling from his mouth. He still wasn't wearing a jacket. My hero.

"What happened to McCain?" he asked Tjaden.

"Fell in the river."

Cliffie smiled at me. "Too bad he didn't drown."

I wondered if Tjaden would do one of his har-de-har-har routines.

Two other people came up behind Cliffie. One was Paddy, Sr., from the bar and the other was Jim Truman, the handyman.

Paddy didn't bother with amenities. He went right over to the canoe and looked down at the girl. He looked over at me. "This looks like somethin' that coon friend of yours might've done."

"We don't even know that it was foul play yet," I said.

"All that blood and it's not foul play?" Paddy said. "You're some goddamned lawyer, you are."

"Any of you ever see her before?" Cliffie said, playing his flashlight on her face.

Everybody took a turn gawking at her. Each shook his head.

"Still think you should look up Darin," Paddy said. "You know how them bucks like white gals."

Jim Truman came up and said, "Paddy, I sure don't know why you're always on that colored boy's case. When he's sober and all, you couldn't ask for a nicer young boy."

Paddy looked disgusted. "You plannin' to go down to Memphis and help out the jigs, are you, Jim?"

Way back before the Civil War, some Iowa farmers used to shoot any slave hunters they'd find. They figured anybody who'd profit on runaway slaves deserved to be shot.

Cliffie smirked. "I'll bet ole Jim here's got a taste for dark meat." Then he looked over and saw Mary coming back our way. "I'll get an ambulance out here. Get her over to the doc's for an autopsy."

I sneezed.

"Aw," Cliffie said, "the counselor's getting a cold."

"C'mon," Mary said, sliding her arm around my blanket-covered body. "I'll walk you up to the road and then I'll go get your car."

"I'll stay warmer if I walk, too," I said.

So we started to leave.

"That's three bodies you've been involved with today,

McCain," Cliffie yelled after us. "If I didn't know better, I'd say our counselor has turned mass murderer."

The walk back was even colder than I'd expected. When we got to the rink, a lot of people came over and asked us about the rumors of a dead girl found in a canoe. It was like a press conference. I was freezing. Mary kept trying to drag me away, telling everybody about how cold I was. But they had just one more question. And then one more. And so on.

She drove to my place. We turned the heater up so far it sounded like a B-52 engine.

She knew just what to do. While I got out of my wet clothes, she was in the bathroom running hot water into the tub. I grabbed a bottle of brandy from the cabinet, a couple of glasses from the kitchen and the portable radio from my bedside.

She said, "Get in. I'll pull up a chair out there and we can talk through the door." She smiled. "That way you can remain modest and virginal."

It worked out well, actually, the water steaming hot and all. I think I invented a few new swear words in that moment of torture when flesh first met water. But I gradually got used to it. I started sipping brandy and then I started feeling warm.

What we talked about was the Knolls and what it was like growing up there and how, for all the poverty and occasional violence, we'd actually had some pretty good times. She made me remember people and moments that came back to me vivid as snapshots. She even brought back certain smells and sounds. She didn't talk about us, not about a romantic us anyway, and I appreciated that because every few minutes Pamela would come into my head. I'd see her or hear her and then Mary wouldn't be there anymore, it would be Pamela.

I stayed in the tub an hour. I had to keep replenishing the hot water supply. I'd get it just hot enough that I could break a sweat.

Then Mary said, "Well, I'd better get going. It's almost nine o'clock. Wes's meeting'll be breaking up pretty soon."

She stood on the other side of the half-opened door. I got a brief glimpse of her beret. "Thanks for taking care of me," I said.

"My pleasure."

We didn't say anything, which was, in its own way, terrible.

"Well," she said.

"Thanks again."

"Sure."

"Maybe I'll stop by tomorrow for lunch."

"Great. Maybe I'll see you then."

"Yeah," I said. "Maybe."

"Well," she said.

"Well, good night."

" 'Night."

I listened to her going down the back stairs. I don't know if footsteps can actually sound sad but hers seemed to. And I, of course, felt like shit. Wes was a pompous ass and what was I doing letting her marry somebody like him? Why the hell did I have to be so hung up on Pamela? I could picture Mary walking home alone, in and out of those pools of light cast by streetlights, pausing on corners like a good little girl to look both ways even though there wasn't any traffic, fetching in her beret and with those earnest brown eyes of hers. She'd walk the two blocks home from here and then a girlfriend would drive her out to get her car at the rink in the morning before work.

I stayed in the tub another half hour. My thoughts drifted to two subjects, the cleatlike soles on the bottoms of Robert Frazier's shoes, and the fact that Susan Whitney had been killed by a .32. Judge Whitney wanted me to prove that her nephew wasn't a murderer—a wife beater, a gambler, a drunk and a bully, yes, but not, God forbid, a murderer.

I watched twenty minutes of *Jack Paar* and then went to bed. I tried to read but I kept dozing off, the paperback falling on my chest. Finally, I clipped the light off and gave in to sleep.

I don't wake up easily. You wouldn't want me as your first line of defense. About the time the Russian Army was marching down Main Street, my eyelids would slowly be opening.

But something woke me. There was winter wind, more November than February, and a shutter next door banging. And there were footsteps. I began to picture one careful footstep after another pressing down on the wooden stairs leading to my back entrance.

I slipped out of bed in the darkness. Both Tasha and Crystal looked seriously disturbed. They tried to cover their fear with yawns but I could tell they were scared.

I wore pajama bottoms. I carried the Louisville Slugger, Mickey Mantle model, that I keep next to my bed for good luck—good luck to split open the skull of any uninvited nocturnal guest.

I crept to the back window. Eased back the shade a quarter-inch. Looked down upon the backyard.

Blue midnight snow. A sentry row of silver garbage cans. A small shed where the lawn mower and other yard equipment is kept, the smell of mown grass intoxicating and powerful inside the tiny shed, a contraband sniff of summer. A narrow alley where tots rode brooms all summer long, said brooms turned into fiery steeds with a child's alchemy.

No sign of anybody. Everything so still, except for the wind-stirred crystals of blue midnight snow, that it might have been a painting.

No sign of anybody.

And then the inching wood-aching sound of secret steps on stairs.

My visitor was working his way up to the door.

I gripped the bat and stood next to the back door, the one he'd have to come through. Surprise is always the best weapon.

Three, four, five, six steps. I decided, given how my calves hurt from my tiptoeing, that I'd probably pass on my next chance to become a ballet dancer. That stuff hurts.

I was at the door. And so was he. The topmost step creaked.

I got my bat ready. I reached out and gripped the doorknob. And then I jerked the doorknob as hard as I could.

Forgetting that it was locked.

That's one of the problems with being awakened from a sound sleep. You don't think clearly.

He heard me, my guest heard me and started down the stairs about eight times faster than he'd come up them. I wasn't going to chase him in pajama bottoms and bare feet.

I ran back to the kitchen window, flung back the shade and looked down on the backyard where my retreating guest was leaving heavy footprints in the blue snow.

No mistaking who he was. There was only one person that big in town who could run that fast: an ex-football player named Darin Greene.

FIFTEEN

AL MONAHAN LOST BOTH his legs on Guam. When he got
home, he took a small inheritance he'd come into and
opened his restaurant downtown. Folks didn't have much hope
for him. Much as they felt sorry for him, and much as they liked
him and much as they appreciated the sacrifice he'd made as their
wartime surrogate, there were already three cafes that catered to
the daytime crowds. But Al surprised them. He could zip around
his restaurant in his wheelchair right smartly, and he was a
damned good cook. It took a year, and a couple of modest bank
loans, but Al finally got the place in the black and eleven years
later had the restaurant where all the local Brahmins chose to eat
breakfast and lunch. Al had one wall fixed up like a war memorial. Everybody in town who'd served in the big war got his photo
on the wall plus newspaper stories citing any medals or awards
he'd won. Al got in a flap with some Korean War vets, Al claim-
ing, like a lot of other WWII vets, that Korea wasn't a war, it was
a United Nations police action, and that they therefore weren't
really veterans of a bona fide war. People figured that he had a
right to his bigotry, having lost two legs in the big war, but Al
wasn't alone. A lot of veterans' groups didn't want to let in Ko-
rean-era vets, either. Al came to his senses one day when the front

door of his place opened up and a man rolled in a wheelchair. Both his legs and an arm were gone, lost in Korea. A few hours later, the man's photo was up on the wall, as well as the newspaper clipping about his purple heart and silver star, and Al had himself a new cook trainee.

Al's was crowded as always. I sat down at the counter and ordered my four pancakes, hash browns, orange juice, coffee and Pepsi. I'm pretty much a Pepsiholic. Mom always says she's surprised I don't take it intravenously while I sleep.

Juanita, the voluptuous farm-girl waitress, took my order and sashayed to the back to call it in, her hips swinging in time to the rhythms of Jo Stafford's cheery "Mockingbird Hill" played low on the jukebox. You would find no rock and roll on Al's jukebox. Al's favorite song was "How Much Is That Doggie in the Window?" He never tired of the dog barking in the bridge of the song. As a culture maven, he's a great short-order cook.

When the voluptuous Juanita brought my coffee, she asked me about falling into the pond last night, and then everybody along the counter joined in, too. The consensus was that I was lucky. A farmer said that there were places in that pond that were twenty-feet deep. Then we started talking about the dead girl in the canoe. Her identity seemed to be a mystery and it was getting on to 7:30 A.M. But they were working very hard—"they" being Cliffie, on the assumption that she was the missing girl.

He was late arriving. Most mornings, he was already here when I took my place at the counter. Not today. He would have been busy with funeral arrangements for his daughter, Susan. But folks out here are creatures of strong habit. I knew a guy who went for a mile walk every morning and he went no matter what, even during a tornado one day. He wasn't hurt, but he'd seen a couple of trees uprooted.

He came in late and took his special place. He wouldn't dare have let anybody else have it.

The smells were good here. Bacon and coffee and pancake batter on the scorching griddle. Al had ventilated the place well. You didn't get much scent of sour grease. The odors were lulling me into grogginess—two nights without much sleep had dulled me considerably; I'm always amazed at how Mike Hammer and those guys do it, go sleepless for days on end, and are keen on lots of sex and violence to boot—and then I looked over at him.

Being the Brahmin of Brahmins, Robert Frazier had his own reserved booth in the back. Every day, the lesser Brahmins trooped back there to pay homage. Occasionally, they'd be asked to sit down and talk. This happened about as often as the Pope said, "Hey, how about a game of craps?"

This morning he was dressed in a homburg and an expensive dark topcoat. I didn't get a chance to look at his shoes until he was about halfway back to his private booth. The shoes were the big cleated mothers he'd worn yesterday at the judge's office, the same shoes he'd worn while paying me a visit yesterday.

I let the lesser Brahmins have at him. They were brief today. They'd walk back there, making sure their sorrow masks were in place, and then let the lies filling their mouths spill forth. How much they'd liked Susan and what a great father he'd been to her and how sorry they were for him. Frazier was reviled but he was also feared. He wasn't actually ruthless, I suppose; he was simply without empathy. If you made a mistake to his advantage—in a business or a personal matter—he'd simply act as business textbooks said he should act. He'd destroyed any number of so-called friends and had done so without any apparent regret. I'd always had the sense that it was all one big poker game to him and there were no personal hard feelings. Not on his part anyway.

They spent twenty minutes with their various genuflections and mea culpas. His grief and rage were there to see and they fed on them: it must have been tasty stuff to many of the lesser Brahmins, Frazier's grief and rage. Maybe he'd know now how they felt when he decided to up the ante and cause a few players to drop out, devastating family bank accounts in the process. Tasty stuff, indeed.

Juanita served him; she was his favorite. He usually looked at her with the great avaricious eyes of the richest man in the valley. You could see him hope he would someday add her pelt to his belt. She'd only started here a couple of months ago. He'd probably dry-runned various approaches already. There would be outright bribery, but that would probably offend her; there would be offering her a job in one of his businesses, but that could mean trouble after he'd sucked her youth dry and she was still there; and there would be the emotional approach, the I'm-lonely approach, though the indignity of such a posture would be impossible for such a proud man to endure. He was, I assumed, still contemplating his line of attack.

But not today.

Today, he paid hardly any attention to her. She took his order and walked away. He didn't even watch her voodoo hips sway magically.

I let him eat his breakfast. For a big man, and especially one so surly, he ate with surprising delicacy. It was like watching a heavyweight fighter with a broken nose and a flattened ear knit doilies.

When I walked over and he raised his head to see who dared to interrupt his after-breakfast cigar, he said, "I don't have any time to talk, McCain."

"You made me do a lot of extra work, Mr. Frazier."

"Work? What the hell're you talking about?" He looked like a cartoon war profiteer, the big Roman senator head with the deep scowl on the wide mean lips, the fat cigar stuck with great disdain in the corner of the mouth.

"My floor. Those shoes of yours left tracks all over the floor. I had to scrub them up."

"I still don't know what the hell you're talking about."

"Sure you do, Mr. Frazier. Sure you do."

We stared at each other a long moment and then he said, "Sit down."

"Thanks."

"I'm going to tell the judge about this, of course. You harassing me like this."

"She'll probably ground me and won't let me have any caramel corn for a week."

"Did I ever tell you how much I dislike you, McCain?"

"No. But I kind of got that message a long time ago."

I sat down. I lit up a Pall Mall. I sat back in the booth and looked at him. And said nothing. It was good cop technique, which I learned at the police academy. Silence frequently makes people more nervous than pointed questions.

"I loved her."

"I'm sure you did, Mr. Frazier."

"And I could see this coming, the way he got when he drank and everything."

"He got pretty bad, no doubt about it."

"So why the hell are you bothering me, McCain?"

I said, calmly, "I wasn't kidding about wiping up those footprints. Do you know how much I hate doing housework?"

Juanita started over toward us, raising her pad for action. Frazier waved her angrily away.

"What is it you want from me?"

"I want to know what you were looking for in my apartment."

"I wasn't in your apartment."

"Sure you were."

He put his cigar in the ashtray and then put his head back against the booth and closed his eyes. He stayed that way for at least a minute. I became aware of all the sounds around me. Cafés are noisy places when you actually sit down and listen to them. Waitresses should wear earplugs, like flight crews.

He raised his head and opened his eyes. He looked at me and said, "I wanted to see if you were the one blackmailing him."

"Blackmailing Kenny?"

"The son of a bitch, whoever it is, has already cost me a lot of money."

"Anybody else know about this?"

"If you mean the judge or that clown Sykes, no. As for anybody else, Susan knew about it. And the blackmailer."

"I take it you know why he was being blackmailed."

"You may not believe this, McCain, but I don't."

"He asked you for money?"

"Yes."

"And you gave it to him?"

"Yes."

"But he didn't tell you anything more?"

He looked at me some more. "*He* didn't ask for money. Susan did."

"And she didn't say why?"

"All she said was that it was something that would devastate our family."

"Did you ask her if she had any idea who was blackmailing them?"

"I did. But she said she didn't have any idea at all."

"Do you know how the blackmailer got the money, by mail, or was it dropped off somewhere?" The private investigator's license I kept up to date was finally getting some real use. It had cost $45 and I was using the hell out of it this morning.

"I don't know any of the details. Not any more than I told you."

"When was the last time she asked you for money?"

"Three days ago."

"And you gave it to her?"

"Yes."

"How much?"

He hesitated. "Do you really need to know that?"

"I may not need to know it but Cliffie will want to know it after I tell him how you broke into my apartment."

He sighed. "You don't have much respect for people's feelings, do you?"

That line, coming from the last remaining robber baron in the valley, seemed more than a little unctuous. But I let it pass.

"How much?"

"Three thousand dollars."

"Making a grand total of what?"

"Eighteen thousand."

"In how long?"

"Fourteen months."

I whistled. "That's serious business," I said.

"I'm wondering if that's what drove Kenny to it. To killing Susan and himself."

"If he did it."

"You don't really think otherwise, do you? Esme is just trying to save her family's name. But, hell yes, Kenny killed her. Who else would have killed her?"

"Maybe the blackmailer," I said. "Or somebody else."

"Like who, for instance?"

I knew I was about to jump into waters far more dangerous than the ones I'd slipped into last night. "A lover."

"You bastard. We're talking about my daughter."

"I realize that, Mr. Frazier. But we're all vulnerable and susceptible to all sorts of things. Especially when we're in the kind of position Susan was in."

"She loved him. Don't ask me why."

"She loved him, true. But she was also miserable." I paused. "If anybody would have been justified in looking for solace somewhere else—"

"I raised her better than that."

No point in continuing on with my questions about Susan. In his mind, she was the eternal virgin.

He looked at his watch. "I have to get over to the funeral home."

"I appreciate the time, Mr. Frazier."

He signed his breakfast tab with a flourish and then glanced at me. "I still don't like you, McCain."

"Well, I'm not thinking of asking you to go dancing either."

"And if I catch you trying to sully my daughter's name in any way, you'll be finished in this town. I absolutely guarantee it."

He moved very well for a big man, getting up fast and angry from the booth without even nudging the table, sweeping his coat and homburg along with him. And then he was gone.

I sat there and listened to some more restaurant noises and smoked my Pall Mall.

Juanita came over. "He looked mad."

"Yeah."

"What'd you say to him, McCain?"

"Just asked him a couple of questions was all."

"Gee, his daughter just died, McCain. You got to learn to go easier on people. Like that time you accused Bobby of siphoning gas from Tom Potter's tractor. You were really mean to him."

"He was guilty, Juanita."

"I know he was. But he's my boyfriend, McCain, and I love him. And he wasn't necessarily responsible for goin' to prison those two times, either."

"He wasn't?"

"No, it was them punks he was hangin' out with. Now he just hangs out with Merle Wylie."

"Merle Wylie? He served five years for attempted murder."

"It was the same with Merle, McCain. He just got in with the wrong crowd, too."

"Yeah," I said, "that must've been it."

She watched me carefully. "I can't always tell when you're bein' sarcastic, but I think you are now. About Merle, I mean. He's a lot nicer'n you think, McCain. When my cousin Dodi got—well, you know—knocked up, Merle knew just what to do. And it was the same when my brother got his motorcycle stolen. Bobby was up in prison then so Merle took over and he found it that night and he gave the guy who stole it two broken ribs."

She was about to do some more extolling when one of the customers called her. "You should be nicer to people, McCain." And then walked away.

T HERE   W A S: THE phone bill, the light bill, the water bill, the car repair bill, the grocery bill, and a letter from a guy I'd represented last year on a stolen merchandise charge. He was writing from prison. He said that he couldn't wait to see me when he got out. I wasn't sure how to take that. As I recalled, he'd blamed me for pleading him down to accepting stolen goods. He could've gotten six-to-eight. He'd been caught with more than $12,000 worth of hot appliances in his basement, along with an assortment of firearms that were definitely a no-no for a felon like himself. I got him two-to-four, but he hadn't been happy with me. He said a really good lawyer would have been able to convince the jury that the stolen merchandise in his basement had belonged to somebody else. About three weeks after he hit prison, his sporadic letters started coming in. Superficially, they seemed to be very happy, chatty letters from grateful felon to happy lawyer. But the way he kept repeating how he was going to look me up when he got out made me extremely nervous, even though he had entrusted the fate of all three of his teenage daughters to me. They had been charged, variously, with armed robbery, armed mayhem, destruction of government property, auto theft and reckless driving. This had been their response to Daddy's parole application being turned down. ABC-TV was going to do a sitcom with them to run right after *Ozzie and Harriet*.

My office was one room with carpeting, a tribute to my failed attempt to make a living as a lawyer in a small Iowa town that already had far more lawyers than it needed. I never stayed any longer than I had to. After reading my mail, all of which went into the waste can, I promptly left.

SIXTEEN

"MAMBO," THE LOVELY PAMELA Forrest said when I walked into the office outside Judge Whitney's chambers.

"Mambo?"

"She's going to New York on vacation and wants to brush up on her dancing. She's got that dance step thing you see on TV all over the floor."

Along with powder for jock itch, gum for your bad breath and salve for your pig's hemorrhoids (you have to live in Iowa to get commercials like that), Mother TV had lately been offering us these big plastic things you put on the floor with dance steps all over them. Just follow the steps and you're the next Fred Astaire.

"She's not in a very good mood, McCain," Pamela said.

"Boy, there's a shock."

"I mean worse than usual."

"Impossible."

"I'm not kidding, McCain. She's really on the warpath."

"Any particular reason?"

"Didn't you see the paper this morning?"

"Uh-uh."

She held it up: Millionaire Kills Wife, Self. The deck below read: Prominent Whitney Family Stunned.

Next to a photo of Kenny was a photo not of Susan but of Judge Whitney. The paper is pretty much Democratic and the judge is the polar opposite. She has written them scathing letters for some of their editorial stands. They love to publish them because, despite her obvious intelligence and genuine erudition, she does sound slightly crazed, especially when she defends the John Birch Society.

"Well, they finally got their crack at her."

"They sure did, McCain. I feel sorry for her."

"I guess I might as well get it over with."

"I'll buzz her."

While Pamela buzzed the judge and asked her if she needed anything, I looked at all the galoshes lined up against the wall across the hall. Iowa winter. It was like being back in second grade, in the cloakroom.

The judge was doing her dance steps, following the long sheet of cheap white plastic laid on the floor. The footsteps she followed were black. Up and back, up and back. She was doing the mambo in her judicial robes. I wondered if Oliver Wendell would have approved. The rumor was he'd preferred the cha-cha.

"What're you using for music?" I asked.

"In my head."

"Ah."

"I listened to three mambo songs over and over last night. I've memorized them. It's like having a portable radio. Except I don't need the radio."

"Clever."

"So what do you think, McCain? Do I look all right?"

As a number of her suitors pointed out, picture Kate Hepburn and you've got Judge Whitney. Physically, that is. Emotionally, Judge Whitney makes Kate seem like a softy. That's why I grinned watching her mambo. In her way, she not only possesses true patrician good looks, she's also cute as hell.

"Cute."

"I look cute?"

"You look cute."

She didn't say anything, but she smiled to herself. Beautiful, she'd heard plenty of times. Cute, not so often. If ever.

"I'm going to do all the nightclubs," her honor said, slightly out of breath. "One of my ex-husbands even got me a front-row table to see Sinatra."

"Just be sure he doesn't beat you up."

"Who? My ex-husband or Sinatra?"

"I was thinking about Sinatra but if you're referring to ex-husband number three, Renaldo, that boy had a pretty bad temper, too."

"It's the Latin in him."

"Not to mention the Scotch."

I went over and sat down and sipped at the coffee I'd swiped from the outer office.

FIVE MINUTES LATER, we got down to work.

She went over and sat behind her desk. She said, "You saw the paper?"

"I saw the paper."

"I'm taking you at your word that he didn't kill her."

"He didn't kill her."

She leaned forward on her elbows and glared at me. "Then when the hell are you going to prove it? I pay you a lot of money."

"Not a lot."

"Well, a lot more than most private investigators get."

"Most private investigators aren't lawyers."

She made a face and slumped back in her leather chair. She reached down and pulled the middle drawer of her desk out. Moments later, she strung a rubber band between the thumb and forefinger of her right hand. Our little game.

She shot the rubber band. I tilted my head to the right. The rubber band missed me by an inch.

"Your instincts are getting better, McCain."

"Thank you. I was worried about that."

"I used to be able to hit you every time."

She picked up another rubber band. This time, she got me square in the forehead. "My second husband wasn't worth a damn at this, either. I could always hit him."

"That's probably what sank the marriage. You lost all respect for him."

"What sank the marriage, my sarcastic friend, was the fact that he was spending my inheritance in very, very foolish ways."

"Ah."

Another rubber band. "Ready?"

"Ready."

She aimed and fired. I leaned to the left on this one but the rubber band glanced off my ear. She smiled. "Nice to see I haven't lost my touch." Then she sat forward again, picked up her package of Gaulioses and had herself a cigarette.

"She was unfaithful," she said. "Susan, I mean."

"She had reason to be."

"I realize that my nephew wasn't exactly a prize, McCain."

"That's very perceptive of you."

"But the fact remains she was unfaithful."

"Not that he ever was, of course."

"There's a difference with a man."

"The old double standard?"

She shook her head. Exhaled smoke. "Not exactly. A man, at least a man like Kenny, wants simple sexual relationships. And lots of them. A woman like Susan, who feels wronged in her marriage, wants an emotional relationship as well as a sexual one."

She picked up another rubber band. This time, she missed me. She did another quick one and hit me.

"We're tied, McCain."

"The tension is on."

"Find her lover and you'll find her killer. I'm convinced of that."

"Somebody was blackmailing her."

"What?"

I told her what Frazier had told me this morning. I also told her about him visiting my apartment.

"What was he looking for?"

"Something to tie me to the blackmail, I guess."

"He thought you were the blackmailer?"

"He seemed to think that was a strong possibility, anyway. He figures the way I nose around this town for you, I picked up something to blackmail Susan with."

"What if her blackmailer and her lover were the same person?"

"I've thought about that, too," I said.

"Then I'd say it's time for you to get your ass in gear," she said. "Wouldn't you?"

"Is that a hint?"

"No, that's an order."

She glared at the newspaper on her desk. "I can't wait until they have to retract that headline."

"You going to sue them?"

"Oh, no. It's not the money. I've got plenty of that, McCain. I'd much rather have them grovel."

Anybody else, the line might have been ironic. She was perfectly serious.

I stood up. She brought her hand up from below the desk. Sneak attack. She got me perfectly. Right on the nose. "I win, McCain. Three to two."

What can I tell you? A sixty-one-year-old woman with four ex-husbands and several fortunes in her past, gloating over an inane rubber band contest.

I turned and started to leave her office. "By the way, I heard Pamela warn you that I was on the warpath. I thought I'd surprise you and be nice."

"I appreciate that."

"But now, I really do want to see some results. And I mean fast, McCain." She smiled sweetly with that elegantly cold face of hers. "Fast."

I started to leave again but she stopped me. "And that girl you found in the canoe last night?"

"What about her?'

"She has something to do with this."

"She does?"

Judge Whitney nodded. For all her foibles and excesses, she had good instincts. "Don't ask me what the connection is yet. But I sense one."

"She's a teenage girl."

"I *know* she's a teenager, McCain. But she ties into this somehow. Trust me."

"The doc's probably done with his autopsy by now. Maybe I'll stop over there."

"Good idea." Then, "You really think I'm cute?"

I smiled. "Yeah," I said, "yeah, I do."

Her grin made her ten years old again, little Esme Whitney sitting in her manse being doted on by Daddy's manservants.

I went out and picked up my galoshes from the hallway where all the other boys and girls had stashed theirs for the day.

SEVENTEEN

I DIDN'T HAVE FAR TO go to find the morgue; it's in the basement of the courthouse.

They try to disguise it as much as possible. There's a nice-looking middle-aged receptionist. There's a waiting area with a plump, comfortable wine-colored couch; a table filled with current issues of magazines; and a coffeepot that's always percolating.

Doc Novotony is a distant relative of Cliffie, Sr., and as such his credentials have been questioned a few times. Exactly what *is* the Cincinnati Citadel of Medinomics, anyway? And exactly where is the Thayer Medinomics Hospital where he interned? The state medical board wouldn't give Novotony his license until he battled them all the way to our state supreme court, which decided, begrudgingly, that Novotony was more or less qualified to practice medicine here. But it was a split decision, with the minority report being pretty scathing.

Cliffie, Sr., installed Novotony as the county medical examiner. Novotony then proceeded to shock everybody by being a pretty decent M.E. with but two failings—anytime Cliffie, Sr., wanted results to come out a certain way, that was exactly how those results came out.

And then there's the matter of how he dresses.

Iowa isn't the equal of Texas in its football fervor but for some folks around here, it comes damned close. Doc Novotony, all 260 pounds and five-foot-six of him, is a good example. No matter what the occasion, and I include funerals here, you almost always see him in his black-and-gold Iowa Hawkeye football jersey and his black-and-gold cap and his black slacks with the thin gold piping down the side. He gets kidded a lot, but apparently not enough to change his clothes.

He came out to greet me after Rita, his secretary, had walked back to tell him I was here. He has psoriasis on one side of his face. It has spread over his hands. He has obligingly dispensed with handshaking. He smelled of death, or those morgue chemicals that I associated with death. They smell the same in the places where they put animals to sleep. I took a cat in once and followed the vet back to his special death room. I wished I hadn't.

"Hear you had a little trouble last night, McCain," he said. Then smiled. "Little skinny-dipping with that pretty Mary Travers, huh?"

Rita shook her head and rolled her eyes. She always looked embarrassed by her boss.

"Too bad you got the eye for Pamela Forrest, McCain," Doc Novotony said. "That Mary's a good-lookin' gal. Plus she's got some nice wheels on her, if you know what I mean."

Rita did some more eye-rolling.

"I just said that to get Rita's goat," he laughed. "Got to liven this place up a little bit." He picked up Rita's package of Chesterfield's and lit one. "I owe you one."

"You owe me a carton," Rita said. This time she shook her head, but I sensed genuine amusement with her boorish boss. He wore you down and won you over. Like professional wrestling: you watched despite all your best judgment.

"I'm here about the girl in the canoe."

"You want to see her?"

"Not especially."

"Oh, that's right, I forgot you've got a queasy stomach." He looked over at Rita. "He shoulda been here to see that guy that fell into that corn grinder last week. Now, there was a mess for you."

"Maybe you could let me borrow some photos sometime," I said.

He grinned. "I don't know why Cliff hates you so much. I think you're pretty funny, McCain. And Rita's always tellin' me how cute you are."

"I've never said that in my life, McCain," Rita said.

"I was just teasin' her again. Hard as hell to get her goat, you ever noticed that, McCain?" Then, he nodded to the back and said, "C'mon."

"I actually do think you're cute, McCain," Rita said as we were leaving. "It's just that I've never said it to the doc here. I like short guys."

"Does that include me?" the esteemed graduate of the Cincinnati Citadel of Medinomics said.

"Oh, yeah," she said, "you just get me all hot and bothered."

"I should fire her someday, don't you think, McCain?"

"Actually," Rita said, "there are two guys in this town I can count on, the Doc here being one of them. And the other one being my cousin. He's never let me down."

The morgue wasn't big. There were six body drawers and two tables. There was a new tile floor and a desk and two military-green filing cabinets. The shades were drawn. Everything was shadowy. Only one of the tables had a body on it, concealed beneath a sheet. I thought of that great scene in *The Invasion of the Body Snatchers,* my favorite movie, where the man sees his duplicate laid out on a pool table—after suddenly pulling the sheet back. Ever since then, Kevin McCarthy has been my favorite actor. And Dana Wynter, his costar, became my favorite actress, gorgeous and elegant beyond compare.

Doc had remarked about my queasy stomach. I guess he figured something was wrong with me for not liking to look at dead people. Or smell them.

When he drew back the sheet, and I got a look at her, all of her, I said, "My God, what did they do to her?"

"Abortion. Bad one. Some butcher."

"Son of a bitch." I was thinking of my sister.

"Cliff, Jr., called the sheriff over in the next county. This is the missing girl. They finally ID'd her because of a long surgical scar on her back. This is her. Sixteen. Melinda Carnes. Her dad's a dairy farmer near Alburnett."

"What the hell did he do to her?" This time, I didn't get sick. I got angry.

"You never know about these amateurs," he said, covering her up again. "They use all kinds of instruments when they try and abort these girls. Some of them know what they're doing, some don't. The worst thing's usually infection. It can kill a girl a few days down the line. But you see a butcher job like this and you wonder."

"About what?"

"About if it was on purpose." He took his Hawkeye cap off and scratched his head.

"Why the hell would somebody do this on purpose?"

His eyes narrowed as he looked up at me. "Maybe he hates women. Or maybe he hates sinners. You know, one of those religious types, figures a girl's got it coming for sleeping around before she's married, and he decides he's gonna help God out a little and punish her right here on earth. So he cuts her up."

"But could this have been an accident?"

"Oh, sure. That's the hell of it. One of these amateurs gets lucky a few times and he thinks he's a doc. But then his luck runs out and he gets frustrated and he panics a little, and boom, the girl hemorrhages and dies. Most cases like this, the cutter gets scared and runs off and it takes the girl a while to die. Only thing that could save her is somebody passing by and gettin' her to a hospital on time. This gal didn't have that kind of luck, unfortunately." He put his Hawkeye cap back on. "Her parents are on their way over to identify her for sure. I'm only gonna show them her face. Figure that's the humane thing to do."

He clipped off the light. We walked back through the cool and shadowy room to the reception area.

Rita was on the phone. Everything still smelled of death. I wanted to leave.

"I'm earnin' my money this week, I'll tell you that," he said as he walked me out into the hallway. "First, Kenny Whitney and his wife and now this."

I thought of what Judge Whitney had said, that somehow the two cases were related. That still didn't make any sense to me.

The doc smiled at me. "I don't know why the judge wanted you to come down here, McCain." He winked at me. "She probably knows somethin' we don't."

"She didn't want me to come over here," I lied.

"Right. You came down here because you like dead people so much." Before I could say anything, "And tell her that as a newly eligible bachelor, I'd love to take her to the Valentine's Ball the Jaycees are puttin' on this year." He was currently separated from wife number three.

"I'll give her the message," I said.

I'd give her the message. And then she'd give me the response, and it'd be one that the doc sure wouldn't want to hear.

I automatically started to shake hands and then I remembered the psoriasis and how he spent his time handling corpses. I just gave him a little wave and got out of there, taking the steps two at a time.

EIGHTEEN

I WALKED AROUND DOWNTOWN FOR ten minutes. The fresh
air restored me. It was sun-golden with life. Quite a contrast
to the bowels of death in the morgue.

I smiled at all the pretty ladies who worked in the various
stores, trapped behind plate glass in their starchy blouses and
fashionable bows. I wanted to set them all free. We'd have a
parade down Main Street. We'd be happy and immortal. It was
like being drunk and I realized it was irrational, some kind of life-
affirming panic reaction to the morgue, but so be it. I doted on
the hitching posts. I was old enough to remember when farmers
still occasionally rode horses into town and latched them to these
posts. I stood in front of the Civil War memorial. I could remember a stirring program Alistair Cooke had done on it for *Omni-
bus* one Sunday afternoon. And how on the local news that night,
they'd read a list of all two hundred boys and men from this
county who'd died in that war. And then I stood in front of the
Methodist church staring up at its looming spire and I felt a
stirring of deity in my irreligious heart. I wanted so badly to
believe and it was with great sorrow that I did not.

And then the exhilaration was gone. I wasn't leading a parade
and I certainly wasn't immortal. I was a hayseed standing on a

hayseed street in a hayseed town and just then a manure wagon lumbered past spewing dung-tinged bits of hay as if to confirm my hayseed status. Maybe I needed to hang out in the morgue more often to appreciate my life. Then the beautiful frenzy was gone.

I walked over to a phone booth and called the hospital where Lurlene Greene worked. She sounded scared when they finally got her to the phone, scared as if I was going to tell her bad news. I felt sorry for her. Her color and her husband had both put her through unimaginable hells.

"I'm sorry to bother you, Lurlene, but I'm trying to find Darin."

A pause. "He didn't come home last night, Mr. McCain." She was whispering. She obviously didn't want to share her business with coworkers. She sounded weary and worn.

"Any idea where I could find him?"

"You know where the Trax is?"

"Yes."

"They serve colored there. That'd be my only guess."

"I'll try it. Thanks."

Her voice got even lower. "You see him, Mr. McCain, you tell him his little daughter is running a bad fever and he should be home where a father belongs."

"I'll tell him, Lurlene."

She was crying, then. "I just don't know what to do no more, Mr. McCain."

I wanted to be back leading my parade down Main Street. I'd have Lurlene and her little daughter in my parade right up front and we'd all be happy and immortal together.

"I'm sorry, Lurlene."

Life is like that sometimes, I thought. But why does it always seem to be like that for the good people instead of the bad ones?

"I better get back, Mr. McCain."

"Thanks again, Lurlene."

I got in the car and headed for the edge of the city that had once been the site of a large railroad roundhouse. There'd been a

lot of Negroes and Mexicans working the railroad in those years
and some of them had stayed on to raise families. Each group had
its own trailer court. The Trax was a tavern that sat right between the two trailer courts. Cliffie always sent his white boys
out there when they were eager to kick a little ass without the
respectable citizens getting too upset. The white boys always
won, being the possessors of badges, guns and billy clubs, but
they never escaped unscathed. They sported black eyes and split
lips and limps for a week or so after each skirmish. Nights, they
hung out in downtown taverns, amusing all their fawning friends
with their tales of derring-do, though being one of two white
cops on a lone Mexican isn't something I'd necessarily want to
brag about.

Years ago, the Trax had been a storage building for the railroad. But when the railroad changed hands right before the war,
and the new company divested itself of a lot of its holdings including the roundhouse and support buildings, the Trax became a
tavern.

A glance at the cars parked around the aging wooden building
told you all you needed to know about the social status of the
regulars. There were even two Model-Ts, one a black box with a
roll-out windshield, the other a black box with the back end
sawn off and a bed of two-by-fours laid in to turn it into a
truck—the kind of clanking, clattering Okie-mobiles you always
read about in Steinbeck. The other cars were rusted-out Chevrolets and Fords that dated back before the war. A number of them
had smashed windows and doors and back-ends. Darin Greene's
Olds was in the back.

When I opened the front door of the place, a variety of smells
and sounds assaulted me, from the brine in which the pickled
pig's feet floated, to the choking heavy odor of cheap cigars. The
men's room wasn't exactly smelling like spring flowers either. It
was like the old joke: it got cleaned once a year whether it needed
it or not. The song on the jukebox was "Work with Me Annie," a
very suggestive black rhythm and blues song that two local
church groups demanded be taken out of the record store. The

darkness was blinding, the only real light being the small display of middle-priced whiskey bottles behind the bar, the light above the shuffleboard table and the jukebox. All eyes were on me and few were friendly. Most just looked curious. I couldn't have looked more like a tourist if I'd been wearing a lime-green short-sleeved shirt and plaid Bermuda shorts and had a camera strap slung around my neck.

I walked over to an open section of bar and ordered a beer. I didn't plan on drinking it. The bartender, who had a series of scars on his face, and who was missing a couple of front teeth said, "I think you took a wrong turn somewhere, my friend."

The men along the bar smiled and winked at one another.

"I'll have that beer, please," I said.

"He's that lawyer," somebody from the shuffleboard table said.

"Lawyer?" the bartender said, sounding concerned.

"Nothing to worry about," I said. "I'm trying to find Darin Greene."

The bartender waved a hand around. "Don't look like he's here, does it? Or do we all look the same to you?"

He got some more laughs and more winks from his customers.

The record changed, the new selection being Ray Charles. You could feel the life force in the place change. He sang "I Got a Woman" but the exuberance of his voice said that he had everything else, too.

"Cliffie send your ass out here?" the bartender wanted to know.

"You call him Cliffie, too?" I asked.

"Yeah. So what?"

"That's what I call him."

"Cliffie and him hate each other, man. This boy is all right. Leastways, he ain't no Sykes."

The speaker was gray-haired old and cheap-beer fat and he sat on a wooden chair near the shuffleboard. He had a cigar butt in a corner of his mouth and a bottle of Hamms in his right hand. He wore dark glasses.

"That's old Earle," the bartender said. "He's blind. But don't be fooled, man. Old Earle knows everything."

"Well, he's right about me and Cliffie. We hate each other."

"That still don't explain why you're out here."

"Looking for Darin Greene. Just the way I told you."

"What you want Darin for? He's a friend of mine."

"Well, for one thing, his wife would like him to come home. Their little girl is running a high fever."

"And for another thing?"

This was the keeper of the Darin gate. You see this all the time in small towns, a man or woman who latches on to somebody important, and appoints himself the gatekeeper. The important person doesn't even know about it sometimes, not at first anyway, but eventually he finds out and comes to appreciate the service. And meanwhile, the gatekeeper, in his own mind anyway, becomes pretty damned important himself. To the bartender, Darin would always be the gleaming high school football star.

"For another thing, I need to ask him some questions."

" 'Bout what?"

"Just something that happened recently."

"I can't put you on to Darin less you first put me on to why you want him."

"He paid me a visit last night."

"Oh?"

"Late last night."

"Oh?"

I had a growing audience. They'd watch me when I was speaking, then they'd watch the bartender when he spoke. Back and forth, forth and back. It was better than shuffleboard.

"I'm just trying to find out why he came to my place."

"Maybe you're mistaken. Maybe it wasn't Darin at all."

"It was Darin, all right. I'm just curious is all."

"Just to find out what he wanted last night."

"Right."

He'd started glancing to his right and that was making me

curious. There was a curtain hanging there. A doorway. In the back there'd be stacks of beer cases and other tavern supplies. There might also be a Darin Greene.

Though it was winter, the bartender wore only a white T-shirt. He kept pawing his black hands on the front of the shirt now. He was nervous. He kept glancing at the curtained doorway.

"You boys make sure he don't move from here."

"Sure thing, Donny," one of the customers said.

"I'll be back."

The curtain setup surprised me. There was a door behind the curtain. When it opened, I could hear the click of dice rolling across the floor.

"C'mon, you motha," an angry colored voice said. "Be good to me for once, you bitch." From his groan, I could tell that the dice hadn't been good to him this time. The door closed.

We just stood there watching each other, the men at the bar and me.

"You don't want to screw with Donny," one man said.

"No?"

The man shook his head. "He don't look like it now, maybe, he's got that little gut on him and all, but he had thirty-two professional fights. He even fought Hurricane Jackson in Chicago one night."

Hurricane Jackson was a legendary slugger who had never quite mastered the art of boxing. What he knew how to do was punch and that had taken him a long, long way, further than his limited skills deserved. If Donny had fought him, he must have had at least a respectable career. I was impressed. Donny's career was a long way from my Golden Gloves glory.

Two things happened at once. Donny came back and a car engine started up. A big car engine. Out back. An Oldsmobile.

"I thought he mighta snuck out the back way," Donny said. "But he wasn't there."

"I see."

"But if I see him, I'll tell him you was lookin' for him."

"I'd appreciate that."

Donny nodded to my beer. "Hate to see a beer wasted like that, man."

"I just remembered something I need to do."

"Well, I'd bet you could hold on here another five minutes, couldn't you? We just startin' to be friends, man." He was trying to stall for time to give Darin a good five-minute head start. He didn't try to disguise his nod to a giant economy-size guy down at the end of the bar. The man slid across the space separating bar from front door. The front door vanished when he took his place in front of it.

Donny the gatekeeper decided to be extra careful for the important man he represented. He gave Darin a *ten*-minute head start for good measure.

NINETEEN

I SORT OF LIKED THE music they played in Leopold Bloom's. Not that I had any idea exactly what it was, classical music not being my preferred form of listening. But this, whatever it was, was nice.

The store was laid out in three sections. The books were up front. The records were in the center. And the home furnishings, all of them expensive and many of them mysterious to a hayseed like me, were at the rear. There were Persian rugs on the floor and large photographs of authors from Gertrude Stein to Jack Kerouac on the walls. I'd really liked *On the Road* but I wondered what a working-class guy like Kerouac would have made of the Renaulds. They'd have a tea for him and show him off as they would a new car and then, when he'd left, they'd talk about him with the easy intimacy of true friends. I'm leery of people who run stores like these. They're unimportant to the world at large, but within their own domain, they are kings and queens, handing down opinions and judgments like hanging judges ordering executions. They'd gone to the University of Iowa, the Renaulds, and were, at various times, working on novels, paintings and musical compositions that would probably be simply too good to ever show the ingrate world. Steve Renauld had come from money and his father had bought him everything but the one thing Steve wanted most—talent.

It was a few minutes before anybody appeared. A wan young woman, pretty in a studied way, came out of the back room. She wore a black turtleneck, black jeans and sandals. Francois Sagan, a writer I liked, had shown Midwestern girls how to look European: get the hair shorn, wear the black clothes and look innocent and world-weary at the same time. It took a certain concentration, no doubt about it, looking that way.

I said, "Is Steve around?"

"He's upstairs doing the books."

"I'd like to see him."

"I don't think I recognize you."

"I buy most of my books down at the bus station."

She didn't know how to take that. Was I joking? It happened to be true. The bus station had large wall racks of paperbacks.

"He really hates to be interrupted when he's doing the books."

"I won't need much of his time."

"God," she said, "you really can't take a hint, can you? He's busy. If you'd like to leave your name and number, I'll have him call you."

She was beginning to irritate me, which took some doing, given how pretty she was.

"Tell him it's about Susan."

"Susan."

"Uh-huh. Susan."

"No last name?"

"No last name."

She seemed to see me for the first time, and looked mightily displeased at the information her eyes were receiving. "That crack you made about buying your books at the bus depot? You weren't kidding, were you?"

I relished her disdain. "Uh-uh. That's where I buy most of my magazines, too."

Just then, the classical orchestra chose to swell up, as if in angry response to what I'd just said.

"I'll go talk to him."

"I appreciate that," I said.

"He won't be happy."

"Life," I said, "is like that sometimes."

She went up and he came down. Quickly. She hadn't been kidding about him being unhappy. He had a gaunt face with little James Joyce glasses and auburn hair too long for his skinny neck and long head. He wore a white starched shirt with a tab collar, a dark vest and jeans. "Just what are you trying to pull?"

"I wanted to talk to you about Susan."

"Susan who?"

I made a face. "C'mon, you can do better than that."

"I know a lot of Susans."

I walked over and picked up a copy of F. Scott Fitzgerald's *The Crack-Up.* "Good book."

"I don't want to talk about books."

"Really?" I said, looking at him. "Usually, you can't wait to give your opinion."

He leaned toward me and said, "Who the hell told you, anyway?"

"Say her name."

"What?"

"Say her name. You owe her that much."

He shook his head. "You bastard."

The front door opened and Eileen Renauld came in. She wore a cape and a beret and a pair of dramatic black pants and leather boots that laced up to her knees. She had large and dramatic features, austere yet imposing. She wasn't as petulant as her husband but he was a few years older and had had more practice. I had no doubt she'd catch up.

She seemed to know instantly that something was afoot. She said, "What's going on?"

I started to say nothing but he said, "He wants to know about Susan."

For just a moment, her dark eyes showed pain and faint embarrassment and I felt sorry for her. When she didn't have Proust to hide behind, she was almost human. But then instead of being the girl from Mt. Vernon, Iowa that she was, she struck a pose. "You wouldn't expect someone like him to understand, would you, Steve?"

"I guess not."

"I saw him at the bus depot one day looking at girlie magazines."

"Yes," I said, "but I had a copy of Ezra Pound inside the magazine."

She whipped off black gloves and slapped them on top of a glass counter that housed rare books.

She walked right up to me. "Why don't you leave?"

"Because I want to find out what happened between them."

She stared at me and shook her head. "What do you *think* happened between them, McCain? Or do you want me to draw you a picture? They had an affair. It wasn't very long, and I doubt it was very worthwhile, but Steve loves French novels and so to him it was very important."

I didn't know which of us to feel embarrassed for at this point. Maybe I felt embarrassed for all three of us.

But she wasn't finished. "She had big tits and a very nice smile and she loved the way he read poetry to her in bed. He used to read poetry to me in bed, too, back when we were courting. He's especially good with e. e. cummings. It's a better aphrodisiac than wine. But then, I'd hardly expect *you* to understand that, McCain."

"Did you kill her, Steve?" I asked.

He did something he shouldn't have. He looked scared. His eyes clung to his wife's for help. I'd rattled him.

"Did he kill her?" she asked. "Of course, he didn't kill her. What the hell are you talking about, anyway? Kenny Whitney killed her."

"You're sure of that?" I said.

"Yes, I am," she said. "Quite sure."

The clerk came back. She wore a fitted gray winter coat. There was something Russian about it, which was probably the effect she wanted. "It's my break time. I thought I'd go get a Danish."

"Fine," Eileen said. "But yesterday you took twenty minutes. Our agreement is fifteen."

The girl's gaze met Steve's. He looked away quickly, not wanting to anger his wife but appearing to be sympathetic to the girl. The girl left.

"You probably guessed," Eileen said, "Steve and she are at the 'eye' stage of their relationship. Nothing serious yet. Just those wonderful little accidental brushes against each other in cramped spaces, and the occasional hand on the shoulder or on the elbow. Nothing overt, as I say. But they're slowly getting there."

"Why the hell you do have to say things like that, Eileen?" Steve said, miserably.

"Because they're true," she said. "And isn't that what we've dedicated ourselves to, Steve? Truth above all? And that's what McCain wants, too, isn't it, McCain? Truth."

I wanted to run out the door. I'd learned far more about their relationship than I'd wanted to. I hated her for being so pathetically strong, and him for being so ruthlessly weak. He was a lot more dangerous than she was. He'd pull you down and destroy you without even understanding what he was doing.

"Anyway," she said, nodding toward the front door and the girl who just left. "She has bad ankles. And that's a moral failing of some kind, don't you think, McCain? Bad ankles? At least Susan had wonderful ankles along with those breasts of hers."

She picked up her gloves from the top of the glass rare bookcase. "I think I'll go make some very strong tea now."

She left, sweeping her cape off as she walked to the back.

"When's the last time you saw Susan?"

"You don't really expect me to talk now, do you, after everything Eileen said?"

"When was the last time you saw Susan?"

Fear was in his eyes again. "Why the hell are you asking me these questions?"

The front door opened. A matronly woman in a fur coat came

in. She moved with ease for a woman of her age and size. She came directly to Steve. "Eileen called yesterday and said my D. H. Lawrence books were in." She smiled at me. She had a nice smile, actually. "They're not for me, they're for my niece, believe it or not. She loves D. H. Lawrence. And she's seen *La Dolce Vita* three times. I guess she's sort of a beatnik. They live in Chicago and her husband's in advertising. He's a beatnik on weekends."

"I'll get the books, Mrs. Beamer."

I waited around, looking at the new Hemingway editions Scribner's had published over the past year. If I ever got money, these were the kinds of editions I would buy. Steve came back but two more customers came in.

There was no point waiting anymore. I walked to the front door. The matron with the D. H. Lawrence books was just ahead of me. "I hope I don't get arrested for having pornography," she laughed.

"I'm a lawyer," I said. "Call me if you need me."

She giggled naughtily.

It was nearing lunchtime. I decided to stop by my folks'. I started to go get my ragtop. Somebody said, "Hey. Hey, you!"

When I turned, I saw the girl from Leopold Bloom's running to catch up with me.

"I overheard what you were talking about with Steve. About Susan Whitney?"

I nodded.

"He had this real battle with her on the phone the day before she died."

"How do you know it was her?"

"Oh, it was her all right. He was obsessed. He called her all the time and threatened her. He couldn't let go."

I thought about what Eileen had said about this girl and Steve. "Eileen thinks you and Steve are about to have an affair."

She laughed. Her face was tinted red from the cold. It was a healthy and appealing red. "An affair? Are you kidding? They both give me the creeps. All that melodramatic artsy-craftsy bullshit." She leaned closer. "She's got a stack of romance novels in the back she's always reading and he's got a bunch of dirty paperbacks. You hear the crap she gave me about a fifteen-minute break? They don't know it yet but this is my last day. I've got a better job in Iowa City."

"Well, good luck, and thanks for telling me that."

She laughed again. "I think it'd be cool if Steve had killed her. At least he would've done *something* with his life. What a douche bag that guy is." Then, "Say, do you know Maggie Yates?"

The name jolted me. I wondered if she knew about Maggie Yates and me.

But she quickly went on. "I saw Maggie and Susan in the store together a few times. You might ask Maggie about her. She's kind of crazy, but I like her."

"Maybe I should look her up."

"You know where she lives?"

"Yeah," I said. "Yeah, I know where she lives."

I should. I'd slept there often enough.

"Thanks for your help," I said.

She gave me a pert little salute, cute as hell, and then turned and walked away. Iowa City already had a million great-looking girls. Why couldn't she stay here?

TWENTY

THE COLORS IN HOUSING developments always get me. Orchid and mauve and puce, among others. Colors I don't associate with houses. The other thing that always gets me is how many TV antennas there are. The houses look as if they're hooked up for direct contact with Mars.

But despite my misgivings about housing developments—little villages whose dynamics Nathaniel Hawthorne would have understood very well—I was glad for Mom and Dad that they had this place. Mom not only got a new place out of the Knolls but also a garbage disposal, a telephone with an extension in another part of the house, a sundeck and a full basement. Dad got a garage, a big backyard and a look of pride when he sat on the small front porch with his can of Falstaff and listened to the Cubs on the radio.

Personally, I like an older house with fewer neighbors. And a lot less excitement. All the people who bought houses out here lived through the Depression, and most of the men fought in the war. So this is nirvana to them. This is what they dreamed of in the years following the stock market crash, and when they were overseas watching their friends die. And so there's an edge of desperation here, everybody always telling one another how lucky they are and how happy they are. Steak is the talisman: a family that can have steak twice a week is in good shape. And these days most blue-collar families can eat steak just about as often as white-collar families. It's as if they're scared it'll all go away if they don't constantly remind themselves of their great good fortune.

Mom and Dad are like that, but not to an obnoxious degree. Every time Mom opens her big new Kelvinator double-door refrigerator, she says, "I just don't know how I got along all these years without it." And whenever she carries a load of laundry down to the basement, she stops and looks at me and says, "I wish my mother'd lived long enough to see my laundry room. She'd just go crazy about it." For Dad, it's the large shop in the basement. No more cold garages on winter nights; no more leaky roofs that rust out tools. Dad's got a regular workshop down there and he loves it. You can smell freshly sawn lumber and hear the table saw whining through wood so new it's sometimes green.

I could smell the soup the minute Mom opened the door. Tomato bisque. Homemade. How could I say no?

Over lunch, I said, "Ruthie isn't here, is she?"

"Ruthie? She's in school." She gave me a funny look for asking such a stupid question.

Mom is pretty. I suppose most boys think their mothers are pretty. But mine really is. Not that there's much of her to *be* pretty. Eighty-nine pounds and five-foot-one. Dad had to win her away from an accountant named Nesmith. Mom always says it was because of Dad's curly red locks. She said he had the most beautiful hair she'd ever seen. Dad always looks uncomfortable when she says that. And then Mom'll get a little teary and talk about what a good man he's been to her all these years and how she just can't imagine what her life would've been without him. They still dance in the kitchen on Saturday nights, the radio playing the old tunes, Benny Goodman and Harry James and Artie Shaw, and still make out in front of the TV and jump up like teenagers whenever one of us kids show up.

"So everything's going all right with her?" I said around a

spoonful of tomato bisque. I tossed the words off, as if I was just making conversation.

But now I'd gotten her curious. "Why wouldn't everything be all right?"

"Just wondering was all, Mom. I saw her over in town a couple of days ago and she looked tired."

"Oh," Mom said. She looked satisfied that I'd explained my curiosity. "It's her grades. You know how hard she studies. She's got a bunch of tests coming up. So she stays up all night. The poor kid."

The phone rang. Mom went to the yellow wall phone. "It's so handy to have a phone in the kitchen."

I smiled.

It was a friend of hers wanting a recipe. Mom consulted a card file she kept. She read it slowly, giving her friend plenty of time to write down each ingredient.

I was getting groggy. The soup and the kitchen-warmth and the slow way Mom was talking made me want to go upstairs and pick up a Ray Bradbury paperback and read for a while and then drift off to sleep, the way I used to in high school. I'd always been in such a hurry to grow up. Now I wondered if high school was the best time I'd ever have.

When she hung up, she came back and sat down, her shoulder-length dark hair showing inevitable streaks of gray, her sweet little face still wrinkle-free. Dad was the one showing his age and sometimes when I looked at him I felt so sad I had to look away.

"What time's her last class these days?"

"Ruthie's?"

"Uh-huh."

"She usually gets out at two forty-five."

"Oh."

"And then heads over to Sheen's."

Sheen's was a clothing store where Ruthie worked two hours after school every day, putting in a full day on Saturdays. Saving for college.

She was watching me. "You know what's funny?"

"Funny weird or funny ha-ha?"

"Funny weird."

"What?"

"That you haven't mentioned anything about Kenny Whitney."

"Not much to mention."

"Doris' husband—Doris down the street here—he's a cop and he says that the judge doesn't think Kenny killed his wife."

"Neither do I."

"You don't? How come?"

I shook my head, finishing up my homemade soup. "I'm not sure. I mean, there's some evidence he didn't—at least it looks like evidence to me—but even before that, I just had the sense he didn't kill her."

"I have to be careful about what I say around Doris."

"Oh?"

"You know, you working for the judge and all."

"Because her husband likes Sykes?"

"Yes. He and the chief go fishing a lot."

"Right. Probably when they should be out doing their jobs."

"I wouldn't know about that. I just mentioned that I have to be careful."

"I know, Mom."

"The judge isn't exactly well-liked by most people, you know."

I stood up and went over and kissed her on the cheek. "The judge? Not well-liked?" I grinned at her. "You must be talking to the wrong people."

"Oh, you," she said. Then took my hand. I'd never noticed her liver spots before. "I wish you'd stop by more often. I mean, we're right here in the same town."

"I know, Mom," I said. "I'll try harder. I promise."

JUDGE WHITNEY SAID, "Blackmail? For what?"

She sat on the edge of her desk, a paradigm of style in her black suit and red blouse, the cut of both vaguely Spanish, a Gauloise going in one slender hand and a snifter of brandy in the other.

"So he never told you about it?" I said.

Irritation shone in her glance and voice. "McCain, you don't seem to understand. Kenny and I never communicated unless it was absolutely necessary. Having him out to the house would be like having Adlai Stevenson over for dinner."

"Heaven forbid."

"Damned right, heaven forbid. Now the Communists are getting smart. They've decided to put up a much more attractive candidate, and with any luck the sonofabitch will win."

"Who's that?"

"Jack Kennedy? The senator from Massachusetts?"

"Ah. He's a commie, eh?"

"Don't mock me, McCain. Of course, he's a commie. All Democrats are commies."

"I'll have to ask Ayn Rand what she thinks of that."

"Ayn Rand?"

"I've got a date with her tonight."

She exhaled smoke dramatically. "What a little turd you can be."

"She wants me to take her bowling."

"Damn it, McCain, people are walking around thinking that a Whitney has committed murder and you're making jokes about Ayn Rand."

I was going to say that I couldn't think of anybody I'd rather make jokes about than Ayn Rand but I decided the judge had probably had enough.

"Susan's the key," she said, walking back around her desk and sitting down.

The rubber bands started a minute or two later, a volley of them. I'd lean my head right, I'd lean my head left. She was doing pretty good, hitting about 60–65 percent of her shots.

"You're getting better," I said.

"Thank you."

"Did you hear what I said about Susan?"

"I heard."

"She's the key. To the blackmail."

"Why Susan? Why couldn't Kenny have been the blackmailee?"

"He was too stupid to be blackmailed. Everything he did, he did in public. And Susan was a very respectable woman until the last few years of her life."

"That's what Bob Frazier wanted everybody to believe anyway."

"Meaning what?" I said.

"Meaning there was always something a little wild about her."

"You have evidence of this, of course? I mean, she ran around a little, slept with a few guys. I'm not sure that's 'wild.' "

"Not evidence," she said, firing off another rubber band. She got me right on the chin. "Instinct."

"Do you know the Renaulds very well?"

She smiled. "Mr. and Mrs. *New Yorker*? The way they always manage to work the magazine into their conversation is amazing. I guess it's what passes for sophistication out here."

"He had an affair with Susan," I said.

"God. He's so—effete. I'm surprised he's even *interested* in women."

"According to his wife, he's quite the hot number."

"Spare me, McCain." Then, "Anything else I should know?"

"Darin Greene paid me a late-night visit."

"The football player?"

"Yes."

"Why?"

"He didn't say. He got scared and ran off."

"What's he got to do with this?"

"Well, he and Kenny were friends since boyhood."

"Yes, just one more reason the Whitneys were so proud of Kenny. I don't have anything against colored people, McCain—I don't have a prejudiced bone in my body—but being *nice* to colored people is one thing but actually having them as *friends* . . ." She shook her robber baron head. "Anyway,

Greene and Kenny had a falling out was my understanding—well over a year ago now, I think—so I don't see what he'd know about any of this."

"Neither do I. But I was curious why he came up to my place so late at night. Then when I went to this tavern where he hangs out, he took off before I could get to him."

She shrugged. "I'm more interested in the abortion girl."

"I don't know why you think that has anything to do with this."

"Same reason I've always sensed that Susan Frazier wasn't the sweet girl her father said she was. Instinct."

"The doc told me it could just as easily have been an accident as a murder. He thinks that both the girl and whoever was helping her could have panicked. The helper runs off, scared, and leaves her there to bleed to death. I don't know what that could have to do with Kenny and Susan."

"Instinct, as I said." And launched another volley. She hit me once, missed three times.

I looked down at the floor around the leather chair I was sitting in. "Who picks up all these rubber bands after I leave?'

"Pamela."

"Ah."

"Why, do you think *I* should pick them up?"

"There's probably something in the Whitney charter prohibiting it, isn't there?"

"You're wasting time again, McCain. Within twenty-four hours, I want to be able to call up the state paper and demand a front-page apology—or I'll sue them and put them out of business. You're the only one who can help me with that, McCain."

I stood up. "I'm back at it right now, your honor."

"Find out who Susan's best friend was. Work on her."

"That's actually what I was going to do."

"And don't bother Pamela on the way out," she said. "I've got her typing something very important." She exhaled more smoke from her Gauloise. "I don't know why you don't give up on her, anyway, McCain. It just makes you look very foolish to the whole town, a young man mooning over a young woman that way. And I'm saying that for your sake, McCain."

"Thanks, Mom," I said.

On my way out, Pamela said, "Did you hear about Stu?"

"He was hit by a train?"

"Very funny. He was named Young Lawyer of the Year by the State Bar Association."

"Goody," I said, and left.

TWENTY-ONE

THE HIGH SCHOOL HAD a program where kids who worked got off at 2:45 instead of 3:15 so they could go to their jobs. They also got credit for having the jobs. A commie would look at it is a sweet but dishonest plan by greedy merchants to get cheap labor. I wondered what Ayn Rand would make of it.

It's funny that at my age, not long out of law school, I was as sentimental as an old man. The girls looked great, shiny and new, and I knew what most of the boys would do, ride around in their cars and then play a little pool or pinball, and then head home for a quick dinner where they would evade every single important question their parents threw at them. God, it all seemed so far away and so wonderful, MGM wonderful, sort of like an Andy Hardy movie except the girls would let you get to third base and you had all those great Dashiell Hammett and Ed Lacy novels to read.

Now, I had responsibilities and people expected things of me and even at my age I could see a few gray hairs on my head, one of the McCain genetic curses.

I sat there and listened to a local station that played rock and roll in the afternoon. I was nostalgic about rock, because it'd changed, too. They played a lot of Fabian and the Kingston Trio and, God almighty, novelty songs like "Pink Polka-Dot Bikini." And then I started thinking about Buddy Holly again and how Jack Kerouac said that even at a very young age he'd had this great oppressive sense of loss, of something good and true vanished, something he could never articulate, something he had carried around with him as young as age eight or nine, maybe when his brother died. I guess I had too, this melancholy, and somehow Buddy Holly dying at least gave me a tangible *reason* for this feeling. Maybe it's just all the sadness I see in the people around me, just below the surface I mean, and the fact that there's nothing I can do about it. Life is like that sometimes.

Ruthie came out the front door as I'd expected. I was parked up the street. She looked preoccupied and didn't see me. She just started walking fast toward downtown, which was three blocks north. It was overcast now and the temperature was dropping and the school seemed shabby suddenly, shabby and old, and the sense of loss I had became anger and I felt cheated then, as if my past really hadn't been all that wonderful, as if I'd made up a fantasy about my past just because I was afraid to face adulthood. Maybe Joyce Brothers, the psychologist who'd won all that money on the TV show *The $64,000 Question* before everybody found out some of it was a fake, maybe she could explain my sudden mood swings. Nobody in this little Iowa town could, that was for sure.

When Ruthie reached the corner of the school grounds, I was there waiting. She got in.

I said, "Did you try that stuff?"

She stared straight ahead. She looked pale and tired. "It didn't work."

"Oh."

"And it really burns down there now."

"Maybe—"

"Just don't give me any advice right now, okay?" She still didn't look at me.

"Okay." Then, "How're you feeling, physically, I mean?"

"I'm too tired to know. Let's just not talk, all right?"

"All right."

"Could I turn that off? Why can't they play anything decent?"

She snapped off the radio. The song had been "The Purple People Eater." Then, "I'm sorry I'm so bitchy."

"It's all right. I'd be bitchy, too."

"I just need to handle this."

"Don't do anything crazy, Ruthie."

"I don't think I'm the 'crazy' type, do you?"

"No, I guess not."

"I've got a couple of girls working on a couple of things for me."

"Like what?"

"I'm not sure. They just both said they could probably come up with something."

"God, Ruthie, didn't you hear what happened to the girl they found last night?"

"Oh, I heard, all right. But it was obviously somebody who didn't know what he was doing."

"You shouldn't let anybody except a doctor touch you."

"It doesn't have to be a doctor. It's not a tough thing to do if you know what you're doing."

"You're scaring the hell out of me, Ruthie."

"My life's over if I have this baby."

"I know, Ruthie. But still—"

"Here we are."

I pulled over to the curb. Sheen's Fashion Fountain was the most expensive woman's apparel shop in town. It was where you bought your girlfriend a gift if it was her birthday or if you'd really, *really* pissed her off.

She opened the door right away. I had one of those moments when she didn't look familiar. Her fear and grief had made her a stranger. I reached over and touched her cheek. "I love you, Ruthie. You know that. I wish you'd let me help you."

"I did this to myself. It's my responsibility."

"You need a ride home tonight?"

"I can ride with Betty."

Betty was one of the older clerks. She drove to work and lived about two blocks from Mom and Dad.

"I know some people in Cedar Rapids," I said. "They may know a doctor there."

She leaned over and returned my cheek kiss. "Thanks. But let me see what my friends come up with first, all right?"

"Just please let me know what's going on."

"I promise."

She got out of the car. I sat there in gloom, gray and cold as the overcast afternoon itself. Then a car horn blasted me. I was in a No Parking Zone and holding up traffic.

TWENTY-TWO

MAGGIE YATES LIVED ABOVE a double garage on the grounds of a burned-out mansion. One of the servants had lived in the garage during the better days of the manse. Now it was rented out as an apartment. Maggie's bike lay against the wooden steps leading up the side of the garage and Miles Davis' music painted everything a brooding dusky color. I had to knock a couple of times in order for her to hear me above the music.

Maggie was dressed in black. Black turtleneck, black jeans, black socks. Her long red hair was, as always, a lovely Celtic mess and her Audrey Hepburn face was, also as always, a lovely Celtic mess of winsomeness and melancholy.

The walls behind her told the story. Photographs of Albert Camus, Jack Kerouac, James Dean, Charlie Parker and Eleanor Roosevelt cover one wall, while album covers of Gil Evans, Jerry Mulligan, Odetta and Dave Brubeck covered another.

Maggie was the town's resident beatnik. She was somewhere in her early thirties, had graduated from the University of Iowa and was holing up here, she said, so she could write her novel. A lot of times I'd pull up outside and I could hear her banging away on the portable typewriter that sits on the table next to a large window overlooking what used to be a duck pond. As yet, she hasn't let me see as much as a paragraph of the book. But she keeps promising that I'll be the first to read it.

She said, "C'mon in. But I better warn you, McCain. My period started today. And you know I just don't like to do it when I'm menstruating."

I tried my best to sound hurt. "You think the only reason I come over here is for sex?"

"Sure," she said. "And that's the only reason I let you in. I mean, I get my jollies, and you do, too."

I guess this was the brave new world Hugh Hefner talks about all the time. You know, frank and open discussions between the sexes about s-e-x. In some ways, I like it. It's nice coming over here and spending a couple of hours in Maggie's bed and then just leaving and going back to my own little world. I usually make it over here once or twice a week. She has a great body. She says I'm the only "civilized" person in town except for Judge Whitney, whom she says is a "fascist." That's why she sleeps with me, she says, me not being one, a dope or, two, a redneck. She won't accept compliments or anything remotely like affection. One time I said to her, "You really are beautiful, Maggie." She said, "Can the crapola, McCain. You're here because you need sex. That's all that's going on here." I always felt cheated. I want to say lovey-dovey stuff, maybe for my sake as much as hers. The lovey-dovey stuff is nice to say even if you don't mean it—or sometimes even if it's being said to you and you know *she* doesn't mean it. It's like having a smoke afterward.

She said now, "I'm in sort of a hurry. Pete Seeger's in Iowa City tonight. I was just getting ready. My ride should be here any time."

I tried very hard not to look at the sweet smooth curves of that body packed into the black sweater and black jeans. Why not combine a little sex with detection? Hadn't *Mike Hammer* shown us the way?

The apartment consisted of a large living room that looked surprisingly middle-class given all the jazz musicians and literary heroes on the walls; a small bedroom with a very comfortable double bed and a kitchen and bathroom big enough for only one person at a time.

"I didn't know you hung out with Susan Frazier," I said.

She was opening her purse, checking her billfold for money. "Oh, I never really 'hung out' with her. She was interested in art so we went to Leopold Bloom's a few times and I explained Picasso and Chagall and Van Gogh to her. I mean, not that I know all that much myself. God, the guy that runs that store is such a pretentious asshole. You ever notice that?"

"No, I never did," I said deadpan. "He's one of my favorite people."

She whipped her head up and giggled at me. "McCain, you're a certified nut, you know that?"

Now, she was at the closet, digging out a heavy coat.

I said, "You know much about her personal life?"

She put her coat on. Looked at herself in a mirror by the door. "What're *you* going to do tonight, McCain? Stay home and watch *Father Knows Best*?"

I'd made the mistake of telling her that TV shows like that were necessary to society because, corny as they were, they gave us a sense of right and wrong. I believed that. She didn't.

A car horn sounded.

"My ride," she said. "Gotta hurry."

"Hey," I said. "Just one question."

"I really am in a hurry, McCain," she said, grabbing her purse from the coffee table.

"She ever tell you she was in any kind of trouble?"

"Just once," she said, as she opened the door and ushered me out onto the tiny porch.

"What'd she say?"

As she was locking the door from the outside, she said, "She called one night pretty drunk and said it was going to be all over town very soon."

"What was?"

Maggie turned and faced me. "She never got around to telling me. She passed out. She couldn't drink worth a damn."

Then I was following her down the stairs two steps at a time, asking her a few more questions.

I half ran after her to the waiting car. Inside was a slim, balding guy who wore sunglasses and a black turtleneck. I hadn't known that Maggie was dating vampires, but I was happy for her. A mordant jazz song could be heard when she opened the door and slid inside. Then song, Maggie and vampire were gone.

I SAT IN the library until five-thirty. Every ten minutes or so I'd go over and try Debbie Lundigan's phone number. I wanted to find out if Susan Whitney had ever talked to her about the blackmail. There was no answer.

I finally gave up on the phone and drove over there. Debbie lived in an old house that had been converted into two apartments, one up, one down. It was actually a big house, but then you needed the extra space to share with all the rats and cockroaches.

Winter dusk. The sky a moody rose and black with bright tiny stars and a bright quarter moon. Frost already glittering on the windshields of parked cars. To reach Debbie's place you had to climb rickety stairs up the north side of the green-shingled house. You could smell the dinner from the ground-floor apartment, something homey with a tomato base.

I was just about to start up the steps when somebody came from the shadows and said, "Who the hell're you?"

At first, I couldn't see him. He was more shadow than substance. He came a few steps closer and I saw him a lot better. He was imposing. The uniform was regulation army but the decorations were anything but. He was a paratrooper, all spit and polish, caged energy and rage. Then he said, "Hey, McCain, you little bastard. I didn't know it was you!"

Finally, I recognized him, too. Mike Lundigan, Debbie's older brother. He'd been a year behind me in high school. He'd enlisted in the army two days after graduating.

"Hey, Mike! How's it going?"

"Just got back stateside last week and came home here fast as I could."

"Where you been?"

"South Vietnam. Ever hear of it?"

"No."

"Our side is fighting the commies over there. Ike's been sending military advisers. I was over there for a year." He grinned around the cigarette he'd just stuck in his mouth. "We're gonna kick their yellow asses, man. In no time at all."

A car swept up to the curb. The passenger door opened. Loud country music poured from the radio. Debbie got out, said good night, closed the door and the car took off.

Mike ran to her. She screamed his name when she saw him and then hurried into his arms. They'd been orphaned the year after she graduated high school; their folks were killed in a car accident. They had good reason to cling to each other.

After a few minutes, they looked back at me. I walked over to them. "Debbie, I've got a couple more questions I'd like to ask you. But how about if I call you a little later tonight?"

Mike shook his head. "Listen, I was going to run down to the liquor store before it closes and pick up a bottle. Why don't you two talk while I'm gone?"

Debbie nodded. "Fine with me."

Mike kissed her on the cheek then shook my hand. "Be right back."

He hadn't been kidding about running down to the liquor store. He took off at a trot, his heavy lace-up paratrooper boots slamming the sidewalk hard.

"You have a cigarette, McCain? Mine are upstairs."

She always said that. Debbie's favorite brand of smokes was OPs—Other People's. She'd been that way since ninth grade. I gave her a Pall Mall and lit it for her.

"Did Susan ever mention blackmail to you?"

"Blackmail? Are you kidding?"

"No. Apparently somebody was getting money from her for quite a while."

"God, she never mentioned *any*thing like that."

"Did Kenny know about the affair she had with Renauld?"

"No. She didn't tell him."

"Could he have found out some other way?"

"He could have. But I don't think he did."

She started stamping her feet a little to stay warm. "You want to go upstairs?"

"I'm almost done."

"I'm starting to freeze, McCain."

"So she didn't mention any blackmail to you?"

"Nope."

"When she ended it with Renauld, did he ever threaten her?"

"Several times. She used to joke that he had a lousy bedside manner. He was in med school for a while, you know."

"Renauld was?"

"At the U of I."

"I didn't know that." I thought of what Doc Novotony had said about the abortionist possibly being a med student who knew just enough to be dangerous. Would that apply to somebody who'd dropped out of med school?

"You ever *hear* him threaten her?"

"No. But she wasn't the kind to lie. And she was definitely afraid of him."

"You're sure of that?"

"Oh, yeah. He's not exactly the most stable guy in the world." She started slapping her mittened hands together. "Now I've got to pee, McCain. C'mon. Let's go upstairs."

"Actually, that's all I needed."

"Good. Because my bladder can't hold out for long."

She was already starting up the steps. "I still think Kenny killed her, McCain. He hated her and he hated himself—the booze had pickled his brains—and that's what happened the other night."

"Thanks again, Debbie. And tell Mike it was nice seeing him."

*   *   *

I WAS TWO blocks from Debbie's when I saw a red police light bloom into bloody brilliance in the gloom behind me. I pulled over to the curb.

Cliffie just about burst out of his squad car. His right hand rode his low-slung gun all the way up to my car.

He peeked in and said, "You happen to catch the news on the boob tube tonight?"

"No. Unlike some people I know, I have to work for a living."

"And I'm talkin' CBS news, McCain, not that local shit they put on around here."

"So what was on the news?"

"The Whitney family was on the news. How shocked the East Coast part of the family is that Kenny went and killed his wife and then killed himself. The CBS news, McCain." He grinned, his dip-shit mustache as obnoxious as always. "So that kinda makes it official, don't you think? Kenny killed his wife and then killed himself. Case closed. And the poor judge—boy, I'll bet she's never been so embarrassed in all her life. You tell her how sorry I am for her."

"I'll be sure to pass that along."

He smiled again. "I'd sure appreciate that, McCain. I sure would."

He started giggling. And then he walked back to his car. The red light was still on. He was one for drama, our Cliffie was, no doubt about that.

I PULLED INTO the driveway. There were no downstairs lights on. Mrs. Goldman was probably at a movie. Even with her new TV set, she still went to the movies regularly. TV just wasn't the same. Besides, she sort of had this movie crush on Jimmy Stewart. She said she'd never liked him, or even considered him very manly, until he started making westerns. The Avalon had a double feature showing last year, the lonely night of the anniversary of her husband's death, so I packed her off to a restaurant for some Chinese food and then we went to the movies, *The*

Naked Spur with Stewart and *Seven Men from Now* with Randolph Scott. Great films and she had a grand time.

I went up the back stairs. Frost shone on the steps. I had to hold on to the handrail. I stopped and looked up at the moon and stars again. I thought of Sputnik and the space program that was going on at the University of Iowa. People like me didn't look quite so foolish anymore, buying science fiction magazines. Except for the ones where green and many-tentacled monsters were ravishing earth girls in bikinis. We probably weren't going to find a race of horny monsters in outer space, ray gun in one tentacle and a Trojan in the other.

I got the back door opened and reached around to flick on the light. A voice said, "Please don't turn on the light."

"Mary?"

"I'm smoking one of your cigarettes. I hope you don't mind."

"Since when do you smoke?"

"Since tonight, I guess."

I closed the door and came into the living room. I could see her now, sitting in the overstuffed chair. She looked small and young. The alley light cast everything in stark patches of wan light and brilliant shadow, like a Humphrey Bogart movie.

I took my coat off and sat on the couch. She took another drag on the cigarette and then started hacking. "I guess I don't know how to smoke."

"Good. It's not good for you."

"You smoke."

"I know. But you're a lot smarter than I am."

"Oh, shit, McCain."

"What?"

"It was awful."

"What was?"

"Tonight. With Wes. At the pharmacy."

"What happened?"

"People told him about you and me. You know, last night. Out in the woods and everything."

"Oh."

"I know you think he's a jerk, McCain. But the way he was raised—his father's a real Bible-thumper and beat him all the time. You should see him in a swimming suit. You can see these old scars and old welts all over his back. He's got some of that Bible-thumper stuff in him. That's the part I hate. But the other part—"

We sat there and didn't say anything for a while.

"You want anything to drink?" I said.

"No, thanks."

We went silent again. I heard cars passing out on the street. A couple of times, light trucks went by and the windows vibrated. The cats came out and looked us over and apparently didn't find us particularly exciting. They went back into the bedroom.

She said, "He cried."

"Tonight, you mean?"

"Yes. After I got done working, he was waiting for me out in back. He was in his car. He told me to get in. Usually, when I make him mad, he kind of shouts at me. But tonight he was quiet. Real quiet. He kind of scared me a little bit, in fact. The way he just kept looking at me. So I got in the car. I was afraid not to. And then he took me for a ride. I don't think he knew where he was going. He was just driving, you know how you just drive around sometimes. And then when we were out in the park and driving by the duck pond, he started crying. Just sobbing. I didn't know what to do."

She frowned. "Then we got out of the car and walked on the hill above the swimming pool. It looks real strange in winter, like ancient ruins or something. Then he finally talked. He told me how much he loved me and that he knew I loved you and knew that you loved Pamela and that he didn't know what to do about it. And then he said that even if I didn't love him now, he was sure I'd love him someday, and that we should still go through with the marriage and pick out a house and plan to have a kid and everything."

"Oh, shit."

"What?"

"You've succeeded in doing the impossible."

"What?"

"He's one of the most pompous, arrogant bastards in the valley and now you've got me feeling sorry for him. His dad beats him, you and I damned near crushed him and now he's willing to marry you even if you don't love him."

"I feel terrible."

"So do I."

"Maybe I love him, McCain, and don't even realize it."

"Maybe."

"God, McCain, what should I do?"

"I don't know."

"I shouldn't be here."

"No, you shouldn't."

"I feel like a whore."

"Oh, c'mon."

"I don't even know if I love you anymore, McCain."

"It'd be easier if you didn't."

"Easier for who?"

I paused. "For all three of us. You and him and me."

"I guess you're right." Then, "I really do feel like a whore, McCain."

I thought of Ruthie saying that. Ruthie and Mary were about as far from being whores as you could get. And yet they didn't seem to believe that.

The phone rang. In the shadows, the rings were loud, ominous. I didn't get it until the fourth ring. The phone was on the cigarette-scarred coffee table along with the new issues of *Playboy* and *Manhunt*.

A voice said, "He wants to talk to you, Mr. McCain." No amenities. Lurlene Greene.

"Where is he?"

"Here. Home."

"Why didn't Darin call me himself?"

"I had to talk him into it."

"I see."

"He's waiting for you."

"He sober?"

Mary was on her feet, pushing her arms into her coat. She gave me a wan little wave and went to the back door. I waved her off, pointing to the chair, indicating she should sit down. I didn't want her to leave in the mood she was in. I felt a surge of affection for her. I wanted to hold her, smell her hair, feel her mouth on mine. Sometimes, I felt just as confused as she did.

"Are you coming out?" Lurlene asked.

Mary left quietly. I went back to the phone conversation.

"As soon as I can. Half an hour, say."

"I don't know how long I can hold him, Mr. McCain. You best hurry." She hung up.

TWENTY-THREE

I WAS HALFWAY DOWN THE stairs before I realized there was a car in the alley. I recognized the new Buick. It belonged to Wes, the pharmacist, Mary's Wes. The engine was running, the parking lights were on. As I reached the bottom of the stairs, I could see two people sitting in the front seat, Wes and Mary.

I felt sick. I wasn't afraid of him, but I was embarrassed for him. I'd followed Pamela all kinds of unlikely places over the years. Sometimes, when I needed to see her, it was like a fever coming over me. I wasn't quite aware of what I was doing. I was all raw need. And then I'd see her and it would be all right. Just seeing her was enough.

There's a kind of symmetry to love affairs ending in cars. That's where most of them start and have since the days of the Model-T. You start out necking and then it gets more serious and then pretty soon you're going all the way. You read a lot of magazine articles about how men are always walking out on women, but I know an awful lot of men who've been walked out on, too. Whenever I hear one sex or the other trying to stake a claim on virtue, I generally leave the room.

They sat there in the alley light, the Buick handsome and imposing, sleek as all hell. You could faintly hear words spoken.

Gentle words. And those hurt more than the harsh ones. A lot of times, you don't mean the harsh ones. You just kind of blurt them out unthinkingly. But the gentle ones, man, those are the killers: the considered words; the I-don't-want-to-hurt-your-feelings words; the final words.

Then the driver's door opened and Wes awkwardly got out of the car and shouted over the rooftop. "C'mon, you son of a bitch, let's get this over with!"

I don't know which surprised me more, that he wanted to fight or that he was sloppy drunk.

He came around the back of the car, slipping and sliding in stumbling drunken anger, throwing his fists up like old John L. Sullivan in the days of bare-knuckle fighting.

"You son of a bitch!" he said.

Mary burst out of the passenger door.

"Wes! Wes! Stop it! Stop it!"

"You son of a bitch!" he yelled at me again. I'd have to teach this boy some new swear words.

I stood next to the garbage cans and watched Mary try to stop him from coming at me. At first, she seemed to do a pretty good job. He put his gloved fists down, anyway. He looked lost and frantic, the way drunks get when the booze is turning ugly in them.

Then he went around her. She grabbed for him but slipped and went down on one knee on the ice.

And then he was there in front of me. His fists came back up and he started swinging. He caught me a square one right on the temple, surprising me. There was some ego involved, too. He was a stuffy man and stuffy men shouldn't be able to throw punches like that.

Mary was screaming at him again and then it was all frenzy because he leaped on me and started choking me. You know how it gets in fights—all kinds of things going on at the same time, little explosions of anger and fear and confusion, the neighborhood dogs suddenly starting to yowl, sweat and blood and snot covering my face. That was when I kicked him in the balls. I

know that's something that heroes never do, take those dirty little
shortcuts that frequently mean victory, but he was too big and I
was not exactly a great fighter. I got him good, real good. He
screamed and then he started to flail backward. Mary grabbed
him to keep him from falling and then he lunged to the right of
her and started throwing up. You never see this in movies, the
vomiting, but a lot of parking lot puking goes on after two
drunks have at each other. Then he went facedown in the snow
and Mary screamed and sank down beside him and started rolling him over so she could see his face. When she got him on his
back, he started crying and it was so miserable, that sound—
those tears went all the way back to his childhood—and I felt like
shit for so many reasons all I could do was walk away, around
the side of the house to my car and drive away and head out for
Darin Greene's place.

TWENTY-FOUR

IN THE SNOW AND moonlight, the trailer court looked snug and cozy. Window lights seemed inviting and the silver flash of TV screens promised fun and excitement. Friday nights like this, *77 Sunset Strip* was on, one of those entertainingly improbable private-eye shows where the hero drives a new T-bird and even nuns throw themselves at him.

Passing the trailers leading to Darin Greene's, I heard babies cry, Fats Domino sing, a couple argue and a car being jump-started.

When I pulled up to Greene's trailer, I saw Lurlene Greene stashing two small children into Darin's battered Olds convertible. I started to pull into a parking spot but Darin slammed out of the trailer and waved me away.

"You don't have no business here, man," he said. "Now get your ass out of here."

"Your wife asked me to come out."

"I make the rules around here."

I glanced over at Lurlene. She was just opening the driver's door of the Olds. Our eyes met briefly but then she looked away and climbed inside. The Olds took a couple tries to start then was rumbling like a prairie train in the middle of the night. Darin

slapped the trunk of the car the way a man would slap a horse's
rump. Lurlene gave the big car some gas, backed out of her parking spot and drove off down the narrow lane between the trailers.

Darin watched her go. He wore a T-shirt and dark pants and
no shoes. He smelled sourly of sweat and whiskey.

I said, "Lurlene said you wanted to talk to me."

"*Lurlene* wanted me to talk to you and that's a whole 'nother
thing, man."

"Why did you and Kenny Whitney have a falling out about a
year ago?"

"Who says we had a falling out?"

"You did, for one." He obviously didn't remember much of
our earlier conversation. "And about a hundred people who saw
you get into a fight down at Paddy's Tap one night. You pulled a
knife on him. And then you had another fight about a week later
and broke out a window over at Russert's bar throwing a beer
glass at him."

"We was just drunk is all." Then he waved me off. "I had
enough of this bullshit, man. I ain't got no shoes on. I'm goin' in.
An' you get the hell out of here and leave my wife alone. You
hear? You leave her alone, McCain."

I hit him with the only weapon I had. And, who knew, maybe
it wasn't a weapon at all. Maybe my guess was totally wrong.
"You ever find that gun of yours?"

He tensed up. No doubt about it. "What gun, man?"

"Your thirty-two."

"I don't know what you're talkin' about."

"Yesterday. When they were throwing you out of Paddy's. I
drove your car, remember?"

"Yeah? So?"

"You said you couldn't find your gun."

"Not me, man. I never had no gun to lose." He'd forgotten
that, too.

"I think I know where it is."

He looked startled. "What you talkin' about?"

"Cliffie Sykes has got it. It's the gun he found at Kenny Whitney's. It's the gun that was used to kill Susan."

He started walking. I don't know where he was going, but he seemed frantic to get there. He must have walked, barefooted in the icy night, four, five hundred feet down that narrow asphalt strip of road. And then he stopped and walked back, the Platters loud about two trailers down.

"I didn't kill her, man. I swear I didn't. A colored man like me, Sykes'd hang my ass for sure if he ever found out that was my gun."

Actually, Sykes probably *wouldn't* hang his ass. He was having too good a time sullying the familial pride of the Whitneys, but I didn't want Greene to know that.

"How'd the gun get out at Whitney's?"

He looked sullen and then he looked sad. "I gave it to Susan. About a year ago or so."

"Why?"

Another sullen look. "This ain't any of your business."

"Why'd you give her the gun, Darin?"

After a time, he said, "Because she was afraid."

"Of whom?"

"My feet're freezin', man."

He started doing a little dance step to impress me with how cold his feet were.

"You can sit in the car."

"Up yours."

"Who was she afraid of?"

He was silent for a time. "Kenny."

"What happened between you and Kenny?"

An old Plymouth pickup truck came down the narrow lane. The man inside waved at Darin and Darin waved back. Inside, his phone started ringing.

"I better get that," he said.

And then he was gone and I knew he'd answered all the questions he was going to. I listened to him slam the door and then bolt it from the inside. He must have had three different kinds of bolts.

I backed out of the parking space. I thought maybe I could find Lurlene, but then I decided she had too much of a head start. Besides, I was worrying about Ruthie again. I hadn't liked the way we'd left it, that a couple of her friends would help her take care of things. That was the trouble with the abortion laws, a subject I'd argued about in law school. The alternative to legal abortion was illegal abortion and that meant a lot of innocent girls dying every year because well-intentioned friends had decided to help them out.

When you came into town from the northeast, as I did, it looked a lot bigger, a monument to Mammon out here on the prairies. We even had a Howard Johnson's motel and restaurant and that was the new place for the more social teenagers to hang out. Not the motel—there was only one motel in town that'd let teenagers shack up, a trucking place out on the highway—the restaurant. It was kind of funny seeing all these hot rods in the Howard Johnson parking lot, chopped and channeled louvered Mercs and street-rods and Bob Mallory's beautiful '39 Ford Phaeton, all those Turbo heads and Johannsen ignitions and extra pots to soup everything up.

I drove up to the edge of the parking lot where there was a pay phone. I called my folks and tried to sound chatty. Then I said, calmly as I could, "I told Ruthie I'd help her on this history test she's got next week."

"Oh?" Mom said. "That's strange. I didn't know you helped her with her tests."

I laughed. "You mean, she's the smart one so why would she want help from me?"

"Well—" Mom said. And laughed, too.

"Is she around, Mom?"

"No. She called and said she was staying at Gloria Spellman's— tonight. Said they'd both be up studying all night."

It wasn't true. I wondered where Ruthie really was tonight. I got scared. "Well, tell her I'll call her in the morning."

"I'll tell her, honey."

"And say hi to Dad."

"I will. Love you, honey."

"Love you, too, Mom."

I drove downtown. The girl-cruise was in full flower. Cars of every description moved slowly along Central Avenue where the theaters and pizza shops and hamburger joints were located—where the girls were located. Up and down, down and up, the cars drove, most of the boys resorting to grins and gawks and graceless waves. That was how the uncool boys handled it, the ones in Dad's car or driving the 1948 Kaiser or the 1950 Henry or an old dog of a Dodge that was rusting into death even while you watched. The kids fit their cars. In my day, I'd maneuvered a 1951 Studebaker with bad steering problems up and down Central Avenue. I had science fiction magazines and Gold Medal paperbacks stacked in the backseat and the only radio station I could get played Lawrence Welk every third song. I'd suffered from pimples, wet dreams, athlete's foot and a secret terror that I'd never really be a man. Women only thought you were cool if *you* thought you were cool—and I knew I wasn't cool.

Things didn't look as if they'd changed much. Three exquisite young blondes were flirting with some guy in a leather jacket sitting inside a cherry-red street rod. There was only room for two inside. He was probably deciding which of the lucky girls he was going to let inside. He was doing this while all the losers (those carrying on in my tradition) drove their clunk-mobiles up and down the street.

I found another outdoor phone. But realized I didn't have the change for a long-distance call. I looked up and down the street. The nearest place where I could get change was the Rexall that Wes owned. At first I ruled it out but then decided he wouldn't be there. He'd be home sleeping it off. Or at Mary's letting her help him sober up.

Jim the handyman was the only customer in the pharmacy when I walked up to the counter. A teenaged girl was working tonight. She handed Jim's package over and said, "Here you go,

Jim. Your animals sure are lucky, the way you take care of them." She smiled when she said it.

"Animals are just like humans to me," he said. "They keep me company since my wife died."

"You must have quite a few," the girl smiled.

When Jim saw me, he said, "Hey, hi, McCain. Tell your folks I'll have that roofing estimate for them by Tuesday."

I nodded. "You'll wait 'til better weather to put it on, won't you?"

He laughed. "I sure will."

I asked the girl for change for a five and she gave it to me. Just as I was turning to leave, I heard noise from the back of the store, boxes tumbling down in a crash. Then a drunken man's voice said, "You think I want you anymore after you've treated me this way? You get the hell away from me and you *stay* away from me. You understand that? You *stay* away from me."

The girl and I stared back there for a long moment.

Then Mary Travers appeared, walking quickly out from between the heavy green curtains that concealed the stockroom.

She walked very quickly to the front of the store. She kept her eyes straight ahead, mortified. She was out the front door in moments.

I went out after her. She was already halfway down the block. I caught up with her, sliding on an icy patch the last few steps. Ever the hot dog, I am. I grabbed her by the sleeve as she kept on walking.

We didn't say anything. Just looked at each other. And then I fell into step, walking.

The night was cold enough to numb your nose. We walked by the town square. It looked cold and lonely. The bandstand had smashed snowballs frozen to its sides. The guy on the Civil War memorial had a real bad case of snow dandruff on his shoulders.

She said, "I really hurt him."

"I guess you probably did."

"And maybe I love him."

"Maybe you do."

For the first time since we'd started walking, she looked at me. "I don't think he ever got drunk before."

"He isn't any better at it than I am."

"No, you're the worst, McCain."

"Thanks."

We walked some more. "Maybe I'm so used to thinking that I'm in love with you—well, maybe I'm not anymore and I don't even realize it." She sounded as if she was trying to solve a particularly difficult math problem. "On the other hand, maybe that's true for you, too."

"Me?"

"Uh-huh. With Pamela."

"Oh."

"That you don't really love her anymore, you just think you do."

"Maybe."

"Oh, hell, McCain, I just never thought it'd be this hard when we were growing up. When you're a little kid, it looks like adults know everything."

"Yeah."

We were on a block of taverns now. Every open door treated us to a different form of music—country-western, rock and roll, pop. You could smell beer and smoke. It was payday money being spent on Friday nights. And spending payday money meant not buying groceries and not buying shoes for the kids and breaking your promise again and again to your wife. You work as a public defender for a year, as I did, you hear about payday money a lot.

"I'm going to marry him, McCain."

"I just heard him tell you he never wanted to see you again."

"He's just drunk and hurt."

"Yeah, I s'pose."

"How's that going to make you feel? If I tell him I'm going to marry him?"

"I'm not sure."

"Will you try and stop me?"

"No."

"That's what I figured you'd say."

"Then you're going to do it?"

"Yeah," she said. "I guess I am."

And then she broke away, running down a dark street, her breath plumes of silver, her near-frail body disappearing in the gathering shadows on the dark side of the streetlight.

"Hey, wait up, Mary."

"Just go to hell, McCain. Just go straight to hell."

And then I couldn't see her anymore, it was almost eerie the way she vanished, I couldn't see her or hear her, she was just gone.

I FOUND A phone booth and got a long-distance operator. It got complicated. I didn't know the number so she first had to call information. By the time we made a connection, my nose was frozen and I really had to piss.

"I'll be damned," a smooth whiskey-voiced man said. He was my age, but sounded ten years older and twenty years smarter. His name was Wyatt Cooper and we'd graduated law school together. He was a Republican, but I liked him anyway.

"You got a few minutes to talk?" We hadn't spoken in six months but the one thing I liked about Wyatt was you could count on him when you were in a spot.

"Well, I've got a friend here. But I suppose she could spare me for a few minutes."

"I appreciate it, Wyatt."

"You think you can keep your hands to yourself for a few minutes, darlin'?" he said.

A female voice giggled in the background and said, "I'll try real hard."

We spent a few minutes talking about the careers of some of our friends who'd journeyed to Chicago and Washington and New York. One of our old cronies had gotten a very good job in

Ike's justice department. He was already working for Nixon's election campaign.

"I'm worried is what I am."

"About what?"

I hesitated. "I know somebody who needs a little illegal medical help."

"You could always get married. I'm thinking of that, myself." I heard the female voice coo in the background.

"I'm not involved. Not directly, I mean."

"McCain, the white knight."

"It's my sister."

"Oh, shit, man, I shouldn't have made a joke."

"It's all right. What I want to know is can you help?"

"Just a sec." He cupped the phone. They talked for several minutes behind his hand. "How far along is she?"

"A month."

He repeated: "A month." Then he cupped the phone again. They talked some more.

"My friend Sue here knows a doctor," he said.

"A real one?"

"A real one. He's a staffer at one of the local hospitals here. Could you get her over to Des Moines?"

"Sure."

"Sue's a nurse. She knows this doc'll help out once in a while if the girl isn't too far gone and if he knows all the people involved. He doesn't want to get his ass in a sling, obviously."

"Is she going to see him anytime soon?"

"Tomorrow morning. They both drew Saturday. She can talk to him then."

"You know what it's like otherwise, without a real sawbones."

"No shit. Girl around here had her friend try it with some kind of automobile suction device. Killed her."

"That's what I'm afraid of. She feels guilty about it and wants to handle it fast before my folks find out. So she might try something stupid."

"I think Sue can have an answer for you sometime tomorrow afternoon."

"That'd be great."

"You still got the same phone number?"

"Yeah. But it'd probably be easier if I called you."

"Fine. Try me around two, three in the afternoon."

"I really appreciate this, Wyatt."

"No sweat. I just hope we can help you out."

NOW I NEEDED to find Ruthie. Her friend Gloria drove a new yellow VW bug that she'd received for her sixteenth birthday from her godfather. I swung by her folks' home. The bug wasn't there. I then began a systematic check of the places where the teenagers hung out. I even drove out to Howard Johnson's again. I spent forty-five minutes on my search and had just about given up when I saw a yellow bug swinging out of the drive of a pizza place out on the south highway.

I honked the horn. Gloria recognized me. I waved and signaled for her to pull over to the curb.

As I approached the car, I could see that Gloria was alone. Would she have any idea where Ruthie was? I felt good about my call to Wyatt. I should have phoned him as soon as I found out Ruthie was pregnant.

Gloria rolled down the VW window and turned down a Frankie Avalon song on the radio.

"Hi," she said. She had a small, freckled face with a slight overbite and a rather pointed chin. She wore a thin yellow parka that almost matched the color of her bug, which I suppose was the idea.

"Hi. I'm looking for Ruthie. Have you seen her?"

I could have won a few million from Gloria in a poker game. Though her lips were shaping themselves into a lie, her eyes glanced guiltily away. "Uh, uh-uh."

"Have you heard from her, then?"

"No, I haven't heard from her, either."

"That's funny."

"What is?"

"My mother's under the impression she's staying all night at your place."

"Gee, that is funny."

I said, "Why don't you turn your engine off?"

For the first time, she showed a little bit of fear. "Why?"

"Because I don't want you to leave until you tell me the truth."

She shifted into first and said, "I'd better be going now."

I reached in and grabbed the steering wheel. "Damn it, Gloria, you remember the girl they found last night? The dead one who'd had the abortion?"

She sank back in the seat.

"Did you hear what I said, Gloria?"

"Yes, I heard."

"You know what's going on with Ruthie, right?"

She took a moment but finally, she nodded.

"Where is she, Gloria?"

She looked up at me. "I don't know."

"Bullshit."

"I really don't. She didn't tell me. She just asked me to cover for her, you know, with your mom, in case she asked if Ruthie was staying at my house tonight."

"Gloria, if she goes to some quack who doesn't know what he's doing—"

"Honest to God, she didn't tell me. She just said she'd figured out a way to take care of it. Honest. That's all she said."

I believed her. Her face had shifted from guilt to exasperation. Now she was telling me the truth and I was acting as if I didn't believe her.

"Do you ever hear of anybody around here who does these operations?" I said.

"You mean like doctors?"

"Doctors or anybody. A nurse, maybe."

"Uh-uh. Most girls go out of state. There's a place in Kansas City where my sister went."

I should've called Des Moines sooner. I could have stopped this from happening tonight.

"If you see her or hear from her—"

"I'll tell her to call you. I really will. But right now I'm kind of freezing my butt off. These heaters—"

"That's all right. Thanks for talking."

"She'll be all right. I'm sure she will."

"I hope you're right, Gloria."

The yellow bug headed up to the corner and then turned right when it got a green arrow on the traffic signal. Mist and fog were setting in. You get a lot of both in the valley. I wondered about my little sister. I should have done so much better protecting her.

I walked back to the phone booth and called Judge Whitney. The brandy was flowing. I could hear it in her voice.

"I hope you've called to tell me that you've found the real killer, McCain."

"Not yet." But I did tell her about my day and some of the strange things that happened.

"Do you think the colored man could have killed Susan, McCain?"

"Possibly."

"Find out why he and Kenny had a falling-out. There might be something in that." She sounded as if she'd just had the most brilliant deductive thought in the world. But I'd been wondering that all day long.

"There's also the fact," I said, "that Renauld was in med school. He might be our man."

"The Leopold Bloom's guy?"

"Yes."

"I wouldn't think he'd have the guts. All the blood. He'd probably say *eek*."

The brandy was flowing indeed. "What's the music playing?" I said.

"You really don't know?"

I let her feel superior as all hell. "I really don't know."

"Why, it's Chopin, of course. I'm very surprised you don't know."

"That question wasn't on my exam when I got my private investigator's license."

"But back to the case. You know who I've also been thinking about?"

"Who?" I said.

"Bob Frazier."

"So have I."

"Really?"

"Between his temper and his pride," I said, "I could see him going out there and killing Susan in a rage. She'd certainly humiliated him enough times in the past couple of years. And Kenny had humiliated him for years. Maybe he just couldn't handle it anymore."

"But then why would Kenny kill himself?"

"Maybe it was the same with Kenny," I said. "In fact, I'm almost sure it was. I was there when he did it, don't forget. He was a very weary and very sad guy. I sensed that he was at the end of things. A pretty good number of alcoholics kill themselves when they feel they're at the end."

"I'm sure I wouldn't know," she said imperiously. Then, "Where are you now, McCain?"

That's when I heard the sirens. Two, maybe three squad cars. That was a lot, even for a Friday night. Once in a while you got that many headed to a single scene if it was a bad accident out on some lonely road. But generally, given the fact that only four cars worked on weekend nights, one car covered most incidents.

"McCain?"

"I'm here."

"Are those sirens?"

"Yeah."

"Any idea what's going on?"

"No. But there's a DX service station that has a police band radio. I'll head over there."

"If it's anything important, you be sure to call me."

"I will."

"I still can't believe you didn't know that was Chopin."

THE DX STATION had glossy promo pictures of Buddy Holly all over the front window. There was going to be a Buddy-a-thon on a local radio station Sunday afternoon.

The place was lit up but I didn't see anybody working. I bought a nickel Coke and some peanuts. I vaguely remembered from health class that peanuts were good energy food. The toilet flushed and the kid came out. He'd apparently been in there dipping his head in an oil can. His long, dark hair glistened with grease. He wore greasy coveralls with the collar turned up. Way up. He looked like Batman.

"Hey," he said.

"Hey."

"You want some gas, daddy?"

Since I needed a favor from him, I decided not to call him "sonny."

"I need your police radio."

"You're that lawyer that works for the judge, right?"

"Right."

"She yanked my license last year for six months. The bitch."

"You were innocent, of course."

"I accidentally bumped this old lady when she was crossing the street. I guess it sort of knocked her down."

"Well, the judge can be unreasonable sometimes, no doubt about it."

"You know the funny thing?"

"What?"

"She's actually a good-lookin' gal."

"The judge?"

"Sure. For an old broad, I mean." He winked. "Maybe if I woulda asked her out, she wouldn'ta yanked my license."

He should have pleaded diminished capacity. "How about the police radio?"

"It don't work too good. In fact, it's shut off right now."

"I'd really appreciate it if you'd give it a try."

He grinned. "You was wonderin' about them sirens, too, huh?"

"Yeah. I love chasin' sirens."

"Me, too, except my chickie, she gets scared when we get over ninety. Her brother was on this motorcycle and he rear-ended this lumber truck and man they had to scrape him off the back end and that's no shit. So ever since, anyway, she gets scared when you hit around a hundred. You know how chicks are."

The front area of the station was a small box with a counter, a twirl rack of state road maps, a red Coke machine, Hawkeye calendars for every sport except marbles, cans of oil stacked neatly along the bottoms of the plate-glass windows and a glass cabinet up on the wall with new fan belts and the like.

"Oh, yeah," I said, hoping that my hands didn't automatically go after this little twerp all on their own.

The kid went behind the counter and produced a long, narrow radio. He plugged it into an outlet that was conveniently set into the countertop. A tiny amber light clicked on in the tuning bar of the radio. "Well, the sumbitch came on, anyway. Sometimes, it won't even do that."

"It won't, huh?"

"Nope. I wanted to take it apart and work on it, but Wally won't let me because of the refrigerator."

"What refrigerator?"

"Oh, you know, the one out in back where the mechanics used to keep their sandwiches and stuff like that."

"What happened to it?"

"Well, me and Merle, he's this friend of mine that Wally don't like much, we spent two nights takin' it apart, you know, tryin' to figure out why it was makin' all that noise, and the damned thing caught on fire." He shook his head. "Sumbitch was just char and ashes."

"That's why Wally won't let you work on the radio?"

"Yeah, you know how Wally is. He took some night classes out to the community college and now he thinks his shit don't stink. You know how college guys are."

He started wrenching the tuning knob back and forth and swearing at it and shaking his head.

"Hey," he said as he continued to twist the knob back and forth, "how about that Buddy Holly, huh?"

"Yeah. God, it was awful."

"You know I bet them guys, them singers, I bet they get more ass than a toilet seat."

"Yeah, I s'pose they do."

He reached in a drawer and pulled out the longest screwdriver I'd ever seen. God only knew what he was going to do with it. He started taking off the back of the radio. "You know what I wonder?" he said.

"What's that?"

"You think any of them singers ever get to screw any of them chicks on *Bandstand*?"

"That I wouldn't know."

"You think Dick Clark ever screws 'em?"

"Most of them are underage."

"Hey, man, that kinda shit goes on all the time in Hollywood. Underage girls, queers, dope addicts, everything, man."

"Yeah, except it's in Philadelphia."

"I thought *Bandstand* was in Hollywood."

"Nope. Philadelphia."

"No shit," he said, amazed at the mysteries of existence. And that's when the radio blasted him back into the big red Coke machine. His screwdriver had discovered electricity. "Whoa!" he said. "You see them sparks! That was really cool! Wait 'til I tell Merle!"

He came back to his radio and said, "Man, this little booger sure got a kick, don't it?"

"Sure seems that way. Well. . ." I said, starting to back up to the door.

"Just a minute, man. Lemme try one more thing. Sometimes, if ya just whomp it a little."

Which was when he started pounding the radio against the edge of the counter. Not a timid let's-try-this-and-see-if-it-works pounding, either. He was really whaling away. I expected to see the radio break into three or four pieces. Instead, it did something phenomenal. It started working.

Myrna Potts, the nighttime police dispatcher, came through loud and clear. "Backup highway patrol car to Kenny Whitney's house on two-two-four-five Pine Valley Road. One more on its way. Repeat. One more backup car on its way."

Kenny Whitney's house? I wondered. Who would be out there now? And why?

"I gotta remember and tell Wally that," the kid said. "Hell, he's got himself a good radio again. Just took a little whompin' is all."

But there was no more time to listen to the sage of the DX. I was out the door and into my ragtop.

TWENTY-FIVE

I DIDN'T KNOW WHAT WAS going on, but it knotted up my stomach pretty fast.

There sat Kenny Whitney's house and in a semicircle around it were three local squad cars, a highway patrol car and an ambulance. Every vehicle had a spotlight trained on the house. Two of Cliffie's deputies had shotguns pointed directly at the place. Cliffie had a bullhorn.

I parked on the hill and walked down the gravel road. There had to be fifty gawkers. They were bundled up and ready for a siege. This was the something you couldn't get on TV. You could smell the jungle thrill on them. This was a doozy, all right.

But why would anything be going on at Kenny's house? He was dead. The house was empty.

Paddy Hanratty, Jr., cleared it up for me.

He'd been standing with his proud father, two dumpy fat guys in hunting jackets, cowboy hats and tumescent bulges of chewing tobacco pressing against their cheeks.

Paddy, Jr., came over, spat right at my foot, barely missing and said, "Looks like we're gonna have us some coon huntin' tonight."

I said, "Care to put that into English?"

He looked truly shocked. "You mean you don't know?"

"Know what?"

"That coon friend of yours, that Greene fella."

"What about him?"

"He broke into the house a little while ago and then managed to get Frazier out here somehow. Now he's got a gun on Frazier and won't let him go 'til he confesses to killin' Susan. He brought Frazier to the winda a while ago and shouted it out to Sykes over there. You know, about Frazier bein' the killer 'n' all."

My stomach got worse. I looked around at the faces of the gawkers and knew what some of them were so excited about now. These weren't the good people of the town; they were the haters. The good people far outnumbered them, but they were not here.

There was likely going to be a killing tonight. That was excitement enough. That the dead man might be an uppity Negro like Darin Greene made the prospect of death even more agreeable.

I stalked away from Jr. and went over to Cliffie. He looked to be in his glory. The bullhorn was a nice touch. The western-style holster rig seemed to ride ever lower on his hips, just the way Wild Bill would have worn it seventy years ago, when he was turning himself into legend.

There was press and they were notably excited, too. Not often small-town reporters get a story like this. This was drama, unlike most of the violence they covered—some farmer killing his wife and then himself in the middle of the night for reasons nobody would ever quite understand, faint, vanished cries lost to the lonely winds around the prairie farmhouse. Three cameras were working constantly, the flashbulb light brief and ghostly.

Up here, at the edge of the driveway that faced the windows of the living room and then dipped below the main floor into the garage, people were passing thermoses around. Apparently, they were expecting a long siege. The sharpshooter deputies didn't take any coffee. They looked reluctant to put their weapons down at all.

Mist and fog and swirling red emergency lights the color of

fresh blood only enhanced the drama. Cliffie had finally gotten himself into a movie.

I said, "I want to go in there."

He'd been sipping coffee from a thermos cup and staring at the house. He turned slightly and took the cup from his mouth. "You think my luck could be that good? Gettin' rid of three of the most obnoxious people in the valley? Greene, Frazier and you?"

"Now that's a responsible comment, Chief. Why don't you share it with the press?"

"Hell, I'm not afraid of those dip-shits. I give 'em a piece of my mind whenever I feel like it. Them reporters don't like any of my family, and I could give a good moose turd."

"I'm serious. I want to go in there."

"For what?"

"To bring them both out alive if possible."

He took another sip of coffee. "I'm not sure you'd be doin' the coon any favors."

"No?"

He shook his head. "Nope. That's not the kind of boy who takes to bein' locked up. And that's where he's gonna be for a long, long time after tonight. Unless he kills Frazier. Then we're gonna hang him, come fall."

"I want to go in there."

"What if Greene decides to kill you?"

"Then he kills me, I guess."

"But you're bettin' he don't because you're such a good friend of the colored." He'd perfected his smirk by the time he was five: it was a masterpiece of malice.

I looked around at the crowd. The decent people of the town, who were in the majority, wouldn't turn out to revel in some-body's grief the way these people had. "I don't see anybody else volunteering to go in there."

"Maybe they've got more sense."

"Or maybe they're just spectators. As long as it's somebody else's blood being spilled, they can just relax and enjoy them-selves."

The smirk again. "Careful now, McCain, you wouldn't want me to tell the press boys your opinion of the common folk, now would you?"

I nodded at the gawkers. "These aren't common folk. These are vampires. They feed on other people's trouble." I was starting to hear some of Judge Whitney's imperiousness in my voice. She didn't particularly like anybody but white Anglo-Saxon Protestants but, by God, she'd defend anyone's right to live and prosper in this country.

"I'd like to let you go in there, McCain. I really would. Because I think Greene'd blow your ass off, but I can't. I'm the chief of police and I've got to use good judgment and good judgment says I can't let you try and pull off some grandstand stunt like that."

I looked at him a long moment, shrugged, then turned and started walking down the gravel driveway to the house.

"McCain! You get back here!" Cliffie started shouting over the bullhorn.

I think he even ran after me a few feet. Then he stopped, as I figured he would. Because even Cliffie could figure out that he really could get rid of Greene and not be charged with anything. If those three or four shots happened to take down the esteemed Robert Frazier, so be it—he was an old fart who'd frequently warred with the Sykes clan, and a rich bastard like him would just make for a juicier news story, anyway.

"You want me to grab 'em, Chief?" one of the deputies shouted.

"Shoot him!" a man in the crowd cried.

"Shoot him good!" cried an older woman.

The fog and mist were heavier as I neared the house. The mist was damp on my skin. The crowd, like a great hungry beast, had roused itself once again, salivating, trembling, shuddering with anticipation. A good evening had now turned into a great one.

A rock caught me on the side of the head. Not a big rock, but one sharp enough and heavy enough to stun me. Several people laughed. I didn't give the bastards the satisfaction of touching the wound to see if I was bleeding. Oh, yes, the beast was definitely roused up again.

The front window was empty. The curtains were open and I could see edges of the couch and an armchair. The rest was darkness. Nobody had reported hearing any gunshots yet so I assumed Greene and Frazier were still alive.

I walked up the six steps that led to the small porch and the front door. I tried the knob. It was locked. I could stand here and argue with Greene to let me in, but that could go on for hours.

I reached in my back pocket and took out my clean, white handkerchief. I wrapped the hanky around my fist and broke out one of the panes in the door window. A buzz went through the crowd. They couldn't see what I was doing. But whatever it was, the sound of breaking glass and all, it had to be exciting. The beast was not only roused, it was excited.

I reached past the jagged remnants of the pane and groped inside for the knob. It turned easily. I pushed the door open and went inside.

Living room. Hallway. Dining room. Dark. It seemed even colder in here than outside. The heat had been off for a while now. I could smell a cold fireplace and stale cigarette smoke. I heard nothing.

I decided there were two likely places Darin Greene would be holed up: bedroom or basement—they would be the most difficult for the police to reach without a shoot-out.

I was going to call out Greene's name but decided against it. He wasn't going to be happy to see me no matter how friendly my voice sounded.

I walked over to the head of the hallway, my footsteps heavy and loud. I was sweating. Maybe Cliffie was right for once. Maybe I was a fool for coming in here. Maybe all Greene would want me for was target practice.

I started down the hallway. More smells came to me. The chemicals the police had used on the crime scene. The seductive hint of perfume, probably from one of the bedrooms down the hallway. And cold—cold has a smell. Jack London always talked about it in his Alaska stories. For the people in his stories, the smell of cold was too often the smell of death.

My footsteps sounded elephantine on the wood floors. I was six, seven steps down the hallway. The light from the front of the house suddenly died. The hallway was very dark.

I didn't really see him until it was over. A silhouette leaned out of a bedroom doorway on the right, near the end of the hallway and two bullets exploded red-yellow from the barrel of a pistol.

I was too busy diving to the bedroom's carpeted floor to recognize who it was. But of course it was Darin Greene. I got a nice rug burn on my chin. Reminded me of the dates I'd had in high school with Pamela. We'd roll around on her folks' new carpeting and I'd get a lot of rug burns but very little else.

"I coulda killed you, man," Greene said from the darkness of the bedroom. "And next time I will. Now you get your white ass outta here."

"Cliffie wants to kill you, Darin," I said, putting a hand against the wall to help me to my feet. "You're making it easy for him."

"All I want is for this son of a bitch to tell me the truth, man," Greene said. "That he killed Susan."

"I didn't!" Robert Frazier half-screamed. "I would never kill my own daughter."

"You found out I was sleepin' with her and you killed her, you son of a bitch!"

So there it was. The reason for the falling out with his old friend Kenny Whitney. There aren't many ways to alienate a man faster than to sleep with his wife.

"Kenny killed her! Kenny killed her!" Frazier said again.

I was scared, but it wasn't a crippling fear. In ninth grade a kid from a county high school picked a fight with me with no warning. It was at a football game and he'd had a few illegal beers. He lunged at me. And I was crippled, paralyzed. I couldn't reach my anger. That's the scariest feeling in the world, when you can't find the wherewithal to fight back. Three or four friends of mine pulled him off me.

Greene fired off a another shot, but all it hit were some perfume bottles lined up along a Hollywood-style makeup table. The bottles sounded delicate as they flew apart. The air was flooded with the high sweet narcotic of expensive perfume.

I rolled past the bed to a place behind a chaise lounge. The bedroom was enormous—the huge canopy bed, the master bathroom off the west wall, two walk-in closets and enough floor space to hold a modest-size meeting.

From behind the chaise lounge, I said, "You don't want to die, Darin. We've got to get you out of this house alive."

"Sykes'll kill me anyway."

"Not if I lead the way out and you've got your hands up. Not even Sykes'd be that stupid."

"He thinks I killed my own daughter," Frazier bellowed. "He called me up tonight and said if I'd come out here he'd tell me who really killed Susan. So, like a fool, I came out here and then he accuses me!"

Greene said, "I know I'm a bastard, Frazier. But I wasn't a bastard to Susan. Believe it or not, I loved her. And she loved me. I was gentle with her. Real gentle. The way I shoulda been with my wife and kids."

Until that moment, I'd had a hard time imagining Darin and Susan together. But the soft way he spoke, I could hear why she'd gone with him, especially considering the way her husband had treated her and all.

Then Darin went and ruined everything.

"You made her get an abortion, didn't you?" Greene said to Frazier. Then he turned to me, "Me 'n' her was gonna have a baby. Kenny couldn't have no kids on account of his sperm count or somethin'. Anyway, she made the mistake of tellin' Frazier here what happened and then he made her get an abortion."

"Yes," Frazier said, "and that's when you started blackmailing her."

Greene hit him. It was one of those blows that you can almost feel; it was so blunt and deadly. I peeked up over the edge of the chaise lounge. Frazier was sinking to the bed. "Don't you ever say that again, man. I loved her and she loved me and I wouldn't blackmail her. No way!"

Frazier, holding his head from Greene's punch, said, "Then who was blackmailing her?"

"I don't know, man. But it wasn't me!"

Frazier raised his head. He looked old now in the spilling light from outdoors, old and baffled and done. Even the anger seemed blanched out of him. "Then you know how I feel when you accuse me of killing my own daughter! I sure as hell didn't like what she was doing. But I didn't force her to have an abortion. She did that on her own. And I didn't kill her, either."

"Where'd she'd get an abortion?" I said.

"She took care of it herself," Frazier said. "At least that's what she told me. Maybe Greene knows."

"No, I don't. She just went and done it's all I know."

By this time, I had crawled to the far end of the chaise lounge. I needed something to throw.

There was a small table at the far end of the chaise lounge. On the table was an ashtray, a star-shaped glass ashtray. It could probably fit comfortably in the palm of my hand. No real weight at all. The only thing that made it a potential weapon were the edges. They couldn't cut deeply, but they could certainly do enough damage to momentarily stun somebody—if the thrower's aim was accurate.

I snatched the ashtray up and gripped it tight. I'd have to stand up to throw with any accuracy. And then I'd have to follow through. Hopefully, between Frazier and I, we could restrain Greene long enough to get his gun. The longer we waited, the hungrier that crowd was going to get.

But the first thing I needed to do was distract him. There was a small cigarette lighter next to the ashtray. That would work.

He went for it. I hurled the lighter against the wall behind him. He whirled. His gun didn't go off, but he yelped, startled, and shouted my name. I took aim and flung the ashtray at him.

"Grab his gun, Frazier!" I shouted as the ashtray left my hand.

So much for my big league baseball fantasies. The ashtray got

him in the neck, not the head. It didn't have the impact I'd hoped
for. He didn't drop the gun, but he did turn toward me and, as he
turned, he was off balance. Frazier moved much faster than I
would have thought possible. He grabbed Greene's gun and then
gave Greene's wrist a savage twist. I came running. None of this
was pretty. Frazier was screaming hysterically, Greene was clum-
sily trying to rain blows on Frazier's head with his free hand and I
stumbled over my own feet as I lunged for Greene. The gun dis-
charged again. My clumsiness saved me.

My momentum continued to carry me forward. I slammed into
Greene and swung a wild punch at his head. It got him in the ear.
I doubt it hurt him much, but it sure pissed him off. And when he
got pissed, he got sloppy. He lunged at me, the gun dangling from
a single finger. Frazier tore it from his hand and then slammed a
punch into Greene's face. He had quite a poke for an older man.
And that was it.

"Now you stay right there, you son of a bitch," Frazier said.
He pointed the gun straight at Greene's face. "I'm going to march
you outside, Greene. And I'm going to make sure nobody hurts
you. I don't want this town of mine to get a reputation for having
a bunch of trigger-happy bigots in it. I'm going to make sure you
get to the jail safe and sound and I'm going to make sure Sykes
treats you right or I'm going to kick his ass from one side of this
state to the other. And I'm also going to see that you get as fair a
trial as possible. And then I'm going to have the satisfaction of
you spending one hell of a long time in a cage where you belong.
You understand me, son?"

Greene just glared at him. It was over for him and Greene
knew it. He seemed smaller now, less menacing, than at any time
I'd ever known him. There was defeat mixed with anger now and
I think even Frazier sensed this. When he spoke again, his voice
was much softer. "I can't stop you from telling people about the
time you spent with my daughter. It won't do her reputation any
good, though, and if you love her as much as you say you do,
then you'll think that over. For her sake." Then, "And for your

sons' sake, too, don't forget. You really want him to know you were in love with some other woman?"

"For *your* sake, you mean," Greene sneered. "Big fancy man like yourself with a daughter sleepin' with a nigger."

"All right then. For my sake. *And* hers. For all our sakes."

Greene glared at him some more. Then he swung his giant head away.

Frazier looked down at his gun. "McCain, you go to the front door and tell Sykes I'm bringing Greene out and if anybody tries anything funny, he's going to answer to me."

"I'll tell him," I said.

I looked at Greene. He was staring at the floor, his shoulders slumped.

I walked down the hallway toward the lights in the front yard. I was thinking about the talk of abortion. Where had Susan gotten hers? And where was my sister, Ruthie, tonight?

The lights in front were stronger now. There were more of them. There were also more people. It was starting to look like a football crowd. Only they didn't want to settle for games. They wanted the real thing.

I crunched pieces of glass as I walked to the front door and opened it. "Sykes!" I yelled before turning the corner where the crowd could see me. I didn't want some yokel thinking I was Greene. "It's me, McCain." I had my hands up.

"Hold your fire!" Sykes shouted over his bullhorn.

I felt stupid, my hands up in the air and all, like one of the guys Robert Stack catches every week on *The Untouchables,* but I kept them there in case one of the more enthusiastic members of the mob got any ideas.

Sykes walked over to me.

"No deals," he said.

"No deals? What deals?"

"No deals with your colored friend."

"Nobody's asking for any deals."

"What was all the gunfire?"

"Nothing much," I said. "The important thing is Frazier's

bringing Greene out. Frazier's got a gun and he's in good shape. He just wants to make sure nobody—the crowd or you—tries anything on Greene."

"Me?" he snapped. "I'm the law here. I'll do what I damned well please."

"That part of the oath you take when you're chief? 'I'll do what I damned well please'?"

But he was already moving away from me, putting the bullhorn to his mouth, instructing everyone to move back, saying that Frazier and Greene were coming out. He also told them not to do anything stupid and to keep their mouths shut when Frazier and Greene appeared. I had to admit, for once he was doing a competent job as a cop.

I headed on to my car up the hill. I wanted to get back to town. I needed to find Ruthie. I also needed to call Judge Whitney and bring her up to date.

A couple of out-of-town reporters rushed me and tried to get me to talk but I just kept on moving. One of them put his hand on my shoulder. I spun around and faced him and he shrunk away. Maybe all those teenage days of trying to look like Robert Ryan were paying off.

I was about twenty yards from my car when I saw a somewhat familiar form emerging out of thick fog. Rita Havers, Doc Novotony's secretary at the morgue. She wore a leather car coat with the collar up and jeans. She also wore a jaunty little golf cap. She was proof that a woman well into her forties could easily still be damned good-looking. Fog encased her like iridescent coils illumined by moonlight, lending her an almost extraterrestrial radiance. The dampness was even worse now. A lot of people with arthritis would be having a bad bone-chilled night.

"Hi, McCain," she said.

"Hi."

"Doc's busy at the hospital so he sent me here to see what was going on. He always counts on me to help him out."

"It's all over."

"Nobody dead?"

"Nobody dead."

She smiled. "Good. Now I can go back home. Jack Paar's got Eddie Fisher on tonight. I'm a big Eddie Fisher fan."

Her earlier words came back. "You said 'he can always count on me.'"

"Uh-huh. Doc Novotony."

"When I was in the morgue, you said that about somebody else."

"I did?"

"Yeah, don't you remember? You said that there was somebody your cousin could always count on. That he never let her down."

"Oh," she said, "yes." Obviously remembering now. "I never should have said that."

"Why?"

"Well, you know. It's family business. Private family business."

"You said she was pregnant and he helped her out."

She shook her head and then looked with sudden longing at the crowd. She wanted to be down there with them. She wanted to be anywhere except here with me, answering questions about private family matters. "I've got to go."

I touched her arm. "This could be very important, Rita. Where did she get her abortion?"

"McCain, look, you're really putting me on the spot here."

"I mean to put you on the spot, Rita. It's very important that I know that name."

She looked longingly downhill to the lights and the crowd. You could tell by a sudden hush that Frazier and Greene had appeared. They hadn't gotten the bloodshed they'd wanted but at least they'd gotten something. A colored man arrested. Maybe Sykes would work him over later.

"Please, Rita. Please help me."

She sighed. "It was Jim."

"Jim?"

"You know. Jim the handyman."

"*He* did the abortion?" The name, the personal style, the way he was perceived by the community—none of it fit. Jim the handyman was Jim the abortionist?

"Yes. She said he laughed about it. How he was a handyman in every sense of the word."

"Jim," I said. "Jim the handyman." I thought of all the medical supplies he'd bought at the Rexall earlier. Maybe they weren't for his animal menagerie. Maybe they were for the girls he aborted.

I kissed her on the cheek and ran back up to my car.

PART III

TWENTY-SIX

THERE'S AN AREA ON the edge of town that reminds me of my one and only trip to beautiful New England. Narrow, spiraling roads with trees set very near the gravel. Hollows that reap fog so thick you can't even see the lights of farmhouses. A lot of dense hardwood forests that glow with the moonlight trapped in the fog that drips from the trees like moss.

I kept the ragtop in second gear all the way. A couple of times, the fog-mazed roads curving abruptly, I nearly ended up in the ditch. I kept the radio off. I needed to concentrate on my driving.

The owl song didn't make the foggy night any cheerier. Nor did the coyote cries. The car continued to grope its way to Jim's.

I slowed down every time I saw a country mailbox, looking for Jim's place.

I used my spotlight on six metal mailboxes before I found the right one. There were no lights buried in the fog. But the box identified Jim the Handyman along with his address.

I pulled the car over to the edge of a gully; I didn't want to turn in the drive, let him know I was coming. I also didn't want anybody to run into it and kill themselves—or damage the ragtop.

I grabbed the flashlight out of the glove compartment. Clicked it on. Nothing. I tried the same trick as the kid at the DX station:

I whomped it against my hand. Light flickered on and off. I whomped it harder. The bulb lit up full glow and stayed steady. This whomping business couldn't be underestimated.

The fog was a damp hand, pressed clammy across my face. I couldn't see three feet ahead. The owl again, and the coyote, and the tramp and crack of my footsteps on gravel.

I started up the drive. I had to sneak in. If he heard me, he might panic and accidentally kill Ruthie. I kept thinking of the poor girl in the canoe.

I'd only been to Jim's once. He had a large frame house with a long, shallow front porch. He had refrigerators and parts of furnaces and lawn mowers and TV sets and all other kinds of junk on the porch. He'd mentioned that these were "dead" items, the ones on the porch, and that he'd be hauling them to the dump soon. He then expressed his displeasure about how the dump was run.

I doubted that any of the dead items had been hauled away as yet. He'd said this four or five years ago. I tramped on. I kept waiting for the outline of the house to impress itself on the shifting fog. But nothing. I was in the netherworld.

It took me a while to reach the house. I knew I was near because of the smells. These were smells of a meal cooked, a tobacco pipe smoked, of oil and metal rust and sweet sawn lumber.

I stumbled on the first porch step. I didn't make much noise, fortunately. I went up the rest of the steps on my hands first, groping, exploring. Far within the house, I heard voices. But they were so muffled, I couldn't tell who they belonged to, or what was being said.

When I was on the porch, I stuck my right hand out and began slowly walking ahead, one careful step at a time. No lights shone from inside. The fog was blinding even on the porch.

I touched a screen door, my fingers running down its coarse surface. The screening was loose enough so that I could push it against the inside door and feel if there was a window. I couldn't remember what the wooden door looked like. It felt like a slab of pine.

If the screen door made noise, Jim would likely hear it. But I didn't have much choice. I stepped back and eased the door open a half inch at a time. Except for a faint thrumming sound made by the spring connecting door to frame, there was no sound at all. I put my hand on the knob of the inside door. It was locked. Great.

I had to go back down the stairs. Though I moved slowly, I still managed to slip on the edge of the mist-covered last step. Somehow, I stayed upright.

I went around the side of the house. The ground was muddy. The exterior of the house smelled of wet wood. My soles made the acquaintance of several plump, juicy pieces of what stank like dog shit. There's nothing like the feeling of your foot telling your brain what you just stepped in.

I had to feel my way around the corner of the house. The fog seemed even more impenetrable back here. For safety's sake, I continued to keep my hands on the house as I made my way across the back. After a few minutes, I bumped into the fruit cellar door. A lot of houses in the Midwest have them. The prairie wives would put up preserves, fruits and vegetables, and pickle certain kinds of meat and then stash them in the fruit cellar, where it was much colder than on the upper floors. A prairie form of refrigeration.

There would likely be steps from the cellar leading up into the house. Sneaking in through the cellar would be easier than getting in any other way. I decided to try it.

I groped my way along the slant of the exterior cellar door. I found a latch. No padlock. I undid the latch and raised the door.

I've never opened a grave so I can't say for sure what they smell like. But the cold and sour rushing odor of the cellar reminded me of dead animals I'd seen rotting in scorching sunlight.

I crept downstairs, following the stuttering beam of my flashlight. There was no flooring, just hard-packed earth. The walls were covered with rotted wooden shelves that held ancient Mason jars containing the sort of indefinable but creepy stuff you see floating in large bottles in carnivals. The ceiling was a crosshatch of electrical wiring. For a handyman, Jim didn't seem to worry much about fires.

A red-eyed rat watched me with malignant curiosity. He probably didn't get many visitors.

I hurried across the wide basement to the sharply pitched wooden steps leading to a door on the first floor. My flashlight chose this moment to go dark.

I set a cautious foot on the bottom step and proceeded to work my way carefully up to the door. I was almost afraid to try the knob. What if it too was locked?

But it wasn't.

I turned the knob all the way to the right and opened the door. A refrigerator motor shuddered on and off; a faucet drip went *pock-pock-pock*. The kitchen.

The voices were louder and clearer now. One of the voices was Jim's. The other's was Ruthie's.

I went left. There was a dining room, or what was supposed to be a dining room. It held four large tables. In the gloom, I could see that appliances of every kind, dozens of them, filled the table. The dust in this room started to make me sneeze. I slapped my hand over my nose and held my breath. I didn't sneeze.

The room where the voices were coming from was on the west side of the house. No wonder I hadn't been able to see the light. I tiptoed to the end of the dining room. A door was outlined in yellow light. Behind the door were Ruthie and Jim.

I moved up to it one slow step at a time. I kept waiting to step on a bad stretch of board—a loud squeak would fill the entire house.

All the time, they were talking.

"You sure you know what you're doing, Jim?"

"If you don't think I can do it, you shouldn'ta come out here."

"Don't get mad, Jim. I'm just scared, that's all."

"I done this when I lived up in Wisconsin and I done this when I lived over to Missouri. I had me a lot of practice, if that's what you're askin'."

He was saying all the right things to convict himself later on. I was glad I'd snuck in rather than barge in.

"All right, Jim. All right." She sounded ready to cry.

"Now you just lie back and we'll get down to work."

Now was the time.

I got myself ready. Took a deep breath. Reached down and grabbed the knob. Prepared myself to charge into the room. And found that the door was locked.

"I'm out here, Jim!" I shouted and started rattling the knob.

He shouted something that I couldn't hear. The lights went out in the room.

"It's my brother!" Ruthie said.

A pistol exploded. He shot through the door. Twice. The sound was vast. I'd been to the side of the door, stripping off my jacket so I could grab him easier when I smashed inside. I hadn't counted on him having a gun.

"No!" Ruthie shouted. "Don't shoot him! Please don't!"

"Shut up, you stinkin' little whore!" Jim shouted.

A moment later, more gunfire. One, two shots. I flattened myself against the wall.

Ruthie screamed at him, "You bastard! Leave him alone!"

"You little slut!" he said.

I heard sliding doors being thrown open, slamming into their respective walls.

"He's getting away!" Ruthie cried.

I finally understood the layout of the house. He had set up his abortion mill in the front parlor and was now going out through the sliding doors that opened on the hallway.

Ruthie turned the light on. I peeked in. He had an old medical examination table in the middle of the parlor and two white glass-fronted cabinets filled with medicines of various kinds.

"Are you all right?"

"Fine."

"I'll be back."

I headed for the door and was immediately confronted by a wall of fog.

I wasn't going to run. It was too dangerous when you didn't know the terrain. But I went after him. Walking steadily, calmly, quietly as possible.

His footsteps receded. I kept moving forward steadily, touching a damp tree here, a fence post there, tactile reassurance that this was reality not nightmare.

And then, somewhere in the fog ahead, I heard a moaning sound. A human moaning sound. A Handyman Jim moaning sound.

"Aw, shit, McCain. You got to help me. I broke my leg real bad."

Not hard to imagine in this fog, tripping and turning your leg into several shards of angled white bone jabbing through hairy flesh.

It took me a few minutes, but I found him. I just followed the cries and the curses. I wondered if the girl he'd killed and put in the canoe had cried this way.

"Here I am, McCain. Help me."

I could see the faint outline of him in the murk. The fog masked some of the pain on his face, but not much of it.

He had the left leg of his Osh-Kosh overalls pulled up. White bone poked through. He kept rocking back and forth and grimacing and tentatively touching his fingers to the exposed bones.

I knelt down next to him and took the ankle of his broken leg and turned it violently to the right. With any luck, his scream could be heard all the way into town. He was sobbing, pleading, almost delirious. "Oh, God, what're you doing, McCain? What're you *doing?*"

Technically, it probably wasn't good police procedure, what I was doing. But it was fast anyway.

It took three leg twists to get it all out of him. How he'd aborted Susan Whitney and then started to blackmail her and killed her with Darin Greene's gun believing Greene would take the rap, but then Kenny had to come along and spoil everything by killing himself with a .45 and making Sykes assume that only a .45 had been used. How'd he'd been operating on the girl I'd

ood measure. I wondered if you had to join a union to be a
sadist. A guy could get to like this stuff.

"I took out the baby. It was a coon. Greene thought she was in
love with him." He snorted bitterly. "Think of that, a jig like
Greene and a upperclass gal like Susan. Them jigs, I tell ya."

"Why'd you kill her?"

He knew enough to answer right away. "I was blackmailing
her. Threatened to tell her father about Darin Greene. She made
three payments was all. Then I went over there one night to get
some more money and she was pretty drunk. She picked the
phone up and said she was gonna call Judge Whitney and tell her
everything, including how I was doin' all these abortions. I guess
I just got mad. She'd threatened me one other time before with
this. I seen where she kept it. I went and got it—and I shot her. I
couldn't believe it. It was like watchin' somebody else do it. Like
it wasn't me at all."

Then, "But I was gonna be real careful with your sister," he
said. "Honest to God, I was, McCain. Honest to God, I was."

Just for the hell of it, I gave his ankle another good twist.

TWENTY-SEVEN

T HE NEXT DAY WAS Saturday and I guess I should tell you about it in sequence. I'll make it as brief as possible.

I woke Ruthie up and we had a long talk and then we went out to the kitchen where Mom and Dad were eating breakfast and told them about her condition. Dad was pretty mad at first but then Ruthie sat in his lap and cried and Dad had a few tears in his eyes as well. Ruthie promised to get the boy over here in the afternoon for a talk with Mom and Dad. And to bring his folks along. Mom and Dad weren't sure how they felt about anything yet. There hadn't been time. Ruthie walked me out to my car and we stood there hugging each other until our noses got cold.

In the afternoon, I stopped by the judge's office and rehashed everything that had happened the night before. She was calling the Eastern branch of her family before I got out the door.

The family name would not be burdened with a murderer after all. Just land swindlers and associated other reprobates disguised as leading businessmen.

In the evening, I went to the Buddy Holly dance. I worked up a good sweat dancing. I danced with anybody who'd have me. Believe it or not, I'm not universally beloved. Around eight, Pamela came in with her date, Stu. I assumed his fiancée was out of town.

He was a whole lot taller than I was and a whole lot smoother with the women and a whole lot better dressed and a whole lot better looking. Other than that, I had no reason to resent him at all.

Mary and Wes came later. Mary looked really pretty in a buff blue sweater and a tight blue skirt and bobby sox and saddle shoes and this really fetching blue bow in her hair. Wes made sure not to look at me. But every once in a while, I'd look over at Mary when they were slow-dancing and I'd feel sad, and I'd just want to hold her, but I didn't know why. I mean it was Pamela I was in love with, but it was Mary I wanted to hold.

Around nine, when they started playing slow songs all the time, I left. I didn't have anybody to pair up with. I started feeling like an outsider, the way I do a lot of times, and so I just went outside and got in my ragtop and drove home and fired up the boob tube and sat on the couch having a Pepsi and letting the cats use me as a bed. There was an Audie Murphy movie on. Being short and Irish, he was a sort of hero of mine.

Audie was just about to shoot all the bad guys when the phone rang. "Yes."

"What're you doing, McCain?"

"Judge Whitney?"

"Of course. Who did you think it was?"

"Is something wrong?"

"Not exactly." I could tell she'd been drinking. "But I need you to come out here."

"To your house?"

She sighed impatiently. "Yes, McCain. To my house. Where the hell else would I be?"

"For what?"

"Just get out here."

THE MANSE IS of red brick. Three stories. White shutters. And white fencing that gives the hundred acres the look and feel of a Kentucky bluegrass horse ranch. Except in the dead of winter.

Her maid, Sophie, a Norweigan woman who is even crankier than the judge, let me in and led me to the den.

Mambo music blared out of a stereo.

The judge wore a festive red blouse and a pair of black slacks and one-inch black heels. Her mambo-lesson footsteps were sprawled all over the floor between the built-in bookcases and in front of the fireplace, black footsteps on a long stretch of white plastic, a brandy in one hand and a Gauloise in the other. And she was following her mambo-lesson footsteps with great fervor.

Sophie gave me her usual frown and left.

"Be with you in a minute, McCain. Help yourself to the dry bar."

I had a beer. From the can. It was my petty protest about being inside the fortress of the master class, as Karl Marx used to call them.

"You could always use a glass," she said.

"Yes," I said. "I always could."

She shook her head with elegant disdain and then went back to her dancing. She was getting good, and she looked good too, in the blouse and slacks.

The music ended.

"Well, get ready," she said.

"Ready?"

"To be my mambo partner. I tried a bunch of other people, but they were all busy. The instructions say that on the tenth night, I should have a live human partner."

"You're kidding. That's why you called me out here?"

"Of course," she said. "Now get over here."

There wasn't any use arguing. I put my beer down, stubbed my Pall Mall out and went over and became her dancing partner.

"God, McCain," she said, when I was in her arms, "I never realized before just how short you are."

As my dad says, life is like that sometimes.